SASHA MASHA

SASHA MASHA

AGNES BORINSKY

Farrar Straus Giroux
New York

Farrar Straus Giroux Books for Young Readers
An imprint of Macmillan Children's Publishing Group, LLC
120 Broadway
New York, NY 10271

Text copyright © 2020 by Agnes Borinsky
All rights reserved
Printed in the United States of America
Designed by Cassie Gonzales
First edition, 2020

10   9   8   7   6   5   4   3   2   1

fiercereads.com

Library of Congress Cataloging-in-Publication Data is available.

Our books may be purchased in bulk for promotional,
educational, or business use. Please contact your local bookseller
or the Macmillan Corporate and Premium Sales Department
at (800) 221-7945 ext. 5442 or by email at
MacmillanSpecialMarkets@macmillan.com

For Chris

SASHA MASHA

Whoever you are holding me now in hand,
Without one thing all will be useless,
I give you fair warning before you attempt me further,
I am not what you supposed, but far different.

—Walt Whitman

I'm grown, and I'm going to wear my dresses.

—Billy Porter

Chapter 1

~~~~~~~~~~~~~~~~~

I grew up in the wrong house. The ceilings were low and there was too much stuff everywhere. Books crammed into leaning bookcases. Blankets folded on the back of the couch. In certain moods I wanted to run away. There are a lot of stories about teenagers who run away. But that always seemed like too much work to me. The teenagers who run away just come back again. And the message of the story is something like, *Why run away when you could learn to be at peace with where you are?* Stories like that didn't help me. I didn't like where I was. It made me itch. Being in that house, alone with my parents, made me itch. Running away seemed like too much work, and I didn't know where I'd go.

You wouldn't know just meeting me that I was the sort of kid who wanted to run away. I got pretty good grades, and grown-ups tended to like me. I could be quiet, but I smiled a lot. If you smile like you understand when people tell you things, they like you. I'd worn the same jacket with a broken zipper since eighth grade. I didn't care about clothes. That's the kind of smiling, nice kid I was.

My best friend was Mabel. Mabel was a badass who wouldn't seem like she'd be friends with someone like me. She was tall—taller than I am—with a thick straight bob of black hair; she would stand there with her head dangling from her neck like a bird. Usually she would hold her hands in her pockets or behind her back, because when she didn't put them away they'd flutter all over the place. We met freshman year and I think she knew right away that I wasn't the person I seemed to be. When I was with Mabel, I would feel a creature wake up in me and run circles around my insides. We used to laugh a lot and go to this coffee place called Carma's, and Mabel would tell me about the girls she had crushes on. I'd laugh and give her advice and then we'd speculate about the future of the world. Coffee was starting to be our big new thing, at the end of sophomore year.

But then Mabel's dad got a job in Pittsburgh and they moved.

Her last night in town we climbed up to the roof of our favorite parking garage. We took pictures of ourselves with the four views behind us—the north, the south, the east, the west.

"Maybelline," I asked her, "what am I going to do without you?"

"Alexidore," she replied, which is what she called me, even though my real name is Alex, short for Alexander, "it's simple. You're going to live your best life and conquer the school."

And we both laughed. We peered down at people who talked with their hands as they waited in line to buy movie tickets or drifted out of the Spanish restaurant. Later we bought a pack of cigarettes to smoke, but they made us sick, so we gave the rest of the pack to a man on a bench. I was sad from that minute on. I get this sadness sometimes that comes over me like a blue shadow, and I got it then. I knew that as soon as the school year started all the teachers would say hello and I'd wave back and smile and people would like me because I was the same person I'd always been—the person they thought they knew me to be.

After Mabel moved, I had about two months of summer left to sulk. I knew other people, yes, sure, but they weren't my real friends. They didn't wake up that little creature inside of me, so why would I want to see them?

I did do one social thing after Mabel left. This was late in July, and the whole city was hot and the Orioles had just won some big tournament, so everyone's cars had flags in the windows. I ran into Jen and Jo, who I sort of knew from our class, in the aggressively air-conditioned produce section of the grocery store, and they said I should come hang out with them sometime. Jen balanced a soda bottle on her head as we stood there. Jo's hands were full of oranges. I could see the goose bumps on their arms from the AC. I was sweaty and I smelled like the sunscreen my mom made me put on. They told me they were going to this pool party at someone's house that night and I should come. They told me Tracy would be really glad if I did. Tracy was the smartest person in our class, with a really nice smile, who I always found a little intimidating.

"Okay, sure," I said, and shrugged.

I didn't know what to make of what they said about Tracy being glad if I came, but Jo pinched my arm until I promised I'd be there.

"I don't know anybody with a pool, so I guess it'd be cool to see what that's like," I said, and immediately decided I sounded dumb.

Jen took the soda off her head; she put her and Jo's numbers in my phone. We parted ways by the tomatoes.

At the pool party, I felt like I kept doing stupid things. I didn't want to take my shirt off because I never liked the way my stomach sagged over the edge of my bathing suit. My chest was pale and my nipples were little soft points. So instead, I ate more chips than I wanted and dripped salsa on the redwood deck. I tripped on the hose at one point and made a weird noise as I fell into the grass. But Jen and Jo and Tracy were nice and made fun of me just the right amount. Even their friend James, who had a buzz cut and an earring and usually made me nervous, seemed like he didn't mind I was there. By the end, I was telling stories about my mom's childhood in North Carolina, on what she always described as a *post-hippie commune*. These were stories I knew would impress people. They weren't about me, but I got to tell them, which meant I got to be at least a little bit impressive. I also told them about this eco-warriors documentary I'd seen. Jen and Jo laughed and came and went with paper plates full of chips and baby carrots. Tracy just sat and listened.

The next morning I woke up knowing I'd been a doofus the night before and decided that none of them would ever want to hang out with me again.

I have this theory that some people are Real People and some people are not. Real People are comfortable being themselves and don't have to think about what they want. They laugh out loud and they eat when they're hungry and they say what they're thinking no matter who is listening. And the paradox of it is that the harder you *try* to be Real, the deeper you know that you're not. Going to pool parties tricks you into thinking you might get to be Real for a little bit. But then you wake up the next morning and you almost don't want to get out of bed because you feel like your body is a costume and your voice is a recording and whatever little kernel of Realness you might have is buried or drowned or dead. That kernel will never, not in a million years, see the light of day.

But maybe that's just me.

I still didn't know what to make of the thing Jen had said with the soda bottle on her head, that Tracy would be glad to see me. Tracy had barely said anything to me during the pool party. And I hadn't said anything to her in particular, just the things I said to everyone. I told my dumb stories and could tell she was listening. At one point I'd asked her what she wanted to be when she grew up. That was something my dad would always say as a joke to other people his age, and it could be pretty charming when he did it, in a dad sort of a way. But I guess it's less obviously a joke when you're saying it to someone who's still a sophomore in high school. Jo had answered for Tracy—jumped in before Tracy could open her mouth.

"Tracy is going to change the world," she said to me, quite seriously.

Chapter 2

The morning of the first day of school, we were all in the auditorium and Dr. Royce was raising his voice over the din. Teachers were waving at former students across the room, some with open mouths and big smiles, others with subdued nods and tugs at their lanyards; Mr. Wolper-Diaz was offering little bows and military salutes. A freshman sat in the broken chair in row *M* and screamed, and everyone laughed because anyone who had been in the school even five minutes knew that the chair in row *M* would dump you on the floor if you tried to put your butt in it.

Dr. Royce used to be a preacher, so when the room settled, we all got ready to listen as he gave us a *sermon*. The message of his sermon was (a) welcome, and (b) you can think of this school as a microcosm of the world, (c) so when it comes to treating each other with respect, (d) every one of you needs to *step up to the plate*. I thought about that phrase for a little while, but I wasn't sure what to make of it. *Step up to the plate.* What did that mean? Work hard? Take initiative? Dr. Royce wore a tailored green suit, and his hands looked big and strong as they gestured or folded over the front edge of the lectern. My sophomore year, there were a bunch of fights and someone got sent to the hospital, so he was probably thinking about that.

I had come in with my homeroom class, and we were all sitting toward the back. Where were Jen and Tracy and Jo? I didn't see them in the section in front of me. To my right was this girl named Caitlin. She was my lab partner in bio last year. She told me she wanted to be a professional dog breeder. We started eating lunch together, but listening to her talk about dog breeds made me want to die. That's when I figured out I could eat lunch in the Spanish classroom if I was nice to Señora Green. To my left was Sabina, who had been president of our freshman class and described herself as a "dynamo." On the other side of her was this weed dealer, Matt. Matt the weed dealer had his arm around Sabina the dynamo, so maybe they were dating. Matt's ex-girlfriend Cierra had once asked me what planet I was from. It made me mad, thinking about that now, it made me feel sad and angry, but generally when I get mad I stuff the anger down inside me. In front of me was Jake Florieau. It's hard to describe Jake as anything besides very gay. We had been best friends for about two months freshman year, but then I went to this concert with him and it turned out there were a bunch of drugs there and my parents found out and I got in trouble, and that was sort of the end of our friendship.

He turned around in his seat. "What's up, Shapelsky?" he said.

"Hey, Jake," I replied. "Not much."

"You ready for a big ol' brand-new year?"

"I guess so."

"You don't seem so excited."

"Eh . . ."

Dr. Royce ran through the demographics of the school, like he did every year. He put numbers on what we all knew already: that we came from different parts of the city of Baltimore, that we had applied to get in here, and that we looked somewhat like the population of the city: a lot of Black kids and Latinx kids and a few Asian kids and some white kids. I was one of the white kids. I had gone to a small Jewish middle school with other white kids. When I finished eighth grade, I was excited to be around people who didn't all look like me. I thought I might learn about other people's cultures, but I mostly learned about my own. I learned how peculiar white people are. White people are stressed about a lot of things and passive-aggressive about a lot of other things. White people want to fix other people's problems but at the same time don't like the feeling of owing anything to anyone. Jewish white is different from Catholic white, of course, which is different from Lutheran white, but you get the idea. Two things that make white people uncomfortable are loud rap music and other people calling them white. Every year at this opening assembly I remembered why I liked going to this school: it made it harder for me to sneak away from who I was. I liked going to this school, I told myself, even though as a junior I still felt like nobody knew me all that well.

Now that I think about it, I wonder if Jake and I hung out just because we were both white. Freshman year, we used to go to these open mics at the One World Café. We'd sit together toward the back and listen and clap and make fun of the stuff that was bad, but then afterward we wouldn't really know what to say to each other. I guess it's depressing, but beyond being white, I don't think we had much in common. I don't know if Jake ever went back to the One World without me. I do know he started making dances. For Spirit Day last year he choreographed something to a really catchy song and did it in purple glitter boots on top of three tables in the cafeteria. I never did things like that. I didn't know catchy songs. I just smiled and did my work and people liked me.

After the assembly we had shortened periods of

English, history, and Spanish, and then lunch. I almost went and sat with Jo, Jen, Tracy, and James—I could see them across the cafeteria, near where the softball people sat—but instead I sat by myself, in the spot Mabel and I used to share. Mabel's first day at her new school was also today. I wondered how it was going. I took a picture of her usual chair and was going to text it to her, but then that seemed a little sad. Instead I texted, "Eep how's day one" with a grimace emoji. When I finished my sandwich I picked every scrap of bread and tuna out of the crinkled sheet of aluminum foil. Mabel texted back right as the bell was ringing. It was a picture of Katharine Hepburn in a safari outfit.

The rest of the day went by in a blur of announcements and handouts, and I was getting my stuff together at my locker when Jen touched me on the shoulder. "I'm having people over for a movie later," she said. "Like seven o'clock. Tracy's coming. You should come too!"

"Okay," I managed to say. I raised my eyebrows earnestly and nodded.

"Text me?"

I nodded again.

"Also, you should tell Tracy you like her haircut."

And she bounded off down the hall.

My dad asked who Jen was, and when I said she was a friend, he winked at me. My dad was always acting like he and I shared some secret. When he did that, I would hold my face really still and not make any expression. His job was to write for the newspaper about Maryland real estate, but I don't think that was ever what he really wanted to do. My mom used to describe him as an eighties dreamer-poet who "gradually made the slide into standard-issue middle-aged male."

"Who also happens to be dazzlingly charming," he would add.

People found my mom dazzlingly charming. She could talk to anyone and was always helping people out. As a social worker at an elementary school, helping people out was sort of her job. I felt like I could tell her most things. But she also worried about me a lot, so I tried to hide it when I wasn't feeling great.

Wherever we went, my parents loved to describe my life to other people, even when I was standing right there. I usually just let it happen.

"I know Alex really loves school," my mom might say to her friend Theresa if we ran into her at the grocery store. "Am I right, sweetie?"

And I would nod and smile and look over at the rows of meat wrapped in plastic.

Or: "Alex is doing really interesting things in history class," my dad might say to his editor if we were stopping by the newspaper some Sunday afternoon. "What was that book you had to read?"

And I would dutifully tell the editor what it was called.

I wondered sometimes if other people's parents were this obsessed with the details of their kids' lives. Certainly Mabel's dad didn't seem to be. Mabel told me once that her dad spent all of her freshman year thinking Mabel loved French. "Maybe after you graduate," he told her, "we can take a trip together to Paris. You can take me around and explain everything to me."

"Dad," Mabel told him, "I take Spanish."

"Oh," he said back. "Why did I think you took French?"

At Jen's I rang the bell and someone shouted, "Come in!"

On the couch inside was a kid I recognized as Jen's older brother, long and sprawled, handsome, in mesh gym shorts. The TV was on, loud, and there was a guy in a baseball cap answering questions while cameras flashed.

". . . very proud of our team this year, our staff, our players, all we've been able to accomplish . . ."

"They're upstairs," he said without looking at me.

". . . we fought through, we're moving in the right direction . . ."

"Cool. Thanks." I hesitated, until his finger indicated the unlit hallway.

". . . that was our goal, goal number one, to get to this point in time, and be able to say . . ."

Upstairs I could hear them all laughing. I knocked lightly on the doorframe of what seemed like their parents' bedroom. Jo's face was very red.

"I'm not saying I want to date him, I'm just saying someone should!" she was insisting. "Hi, Alex! Okay, conversation over."

Jo stood up to hug me, and Jen and Tracy just shuffled over on the couch. There was a king-size bed at the far end of the room, neatly made, covered in pillows. Jen pulled a hair tie off her wrist and redid her ponytail while she clarified that they were talking about Mr. Simon, the drama teacher who'd just started this year and who everyone apparently had a crush on.

People used to say that Jo, Jen, and Tracy looked like they belonged on the cover of a booklet advertising some college that wanted to show how diverse it was. They had been inseparable since freshman year. Jo was half-Korean, Jen was white, and Tracy was Black.

Tracy spoke to me for the first time since the pool party. "Hey, Alex," she said.

"Hey, Tracy," I said back. "I like your haircut."

She thanked me and ran her fingers over the outer

edge of her halo of hair. Her nails were painted a light blue, and her skin was smooth and shining. She had her usual expression—just on the edge of a smile, knowing and a little intimidating.

The room waited for me to sit next to her, so I did. She smelled like the Tibetan store downtown; she smelled like comfort. When Jen turned out the lights and started the movie on the big flatscreen TV, Tracy leaned slightly toward me and her arm pressed against mine. The movie was about a woman who falls in love with a sentimental banker who turns out to be a vampire. I liked the feeling of another body beside me. And I liked that it was Tracy's. I felt comfortable and dizzy at the same time, like I was sinking into bed and also flying.

It felt strange to be sitting next to this person who'd always intimidated me. I did well in school, but mostly it was because I worked really hard. Tracy worked really hard and was also probably a genius. She was the only girl on the debate team, and last year she was ranked second in the state.

Then my nose started bleeding.

"What's up, Alex?"

"Ummm . . . Sorry, everybody . . ."

Jen jumped up from the couch to take me to the hall bathroom. She left me there while I rinsed the blood off my hands and held a wad of toilet paper against my face. I stood there staring at the blue wallpaper, waiting for the bleeding to stop. I could hear them talking through the wall, waiting for me.

After a minute or two, I heard a gentle knocking on the door.

"Hey, Alex?"

"Yeah?"

"Is it okay if I come in?"

"Sure."

I opened the door. Tracy stepped just over the threshold.

"I'm checking on you. Everything okay?"

"Yeah, just a nosebleed."

"I hate that."

"Yeah."

"I have a dry constitution, too. My skin is always cracking." She laughed.

"I think I'm doing this right," I said, in a tiny, muffled voice, as I pinched my nostrils through the toilet paper.

"Just don't tilt your head back. Just pinch. Yeah. It's chilly in here!" She shivered.

"You can come in if you want," I said, and she stepped in farther. She closed the door.

I separated my nose from the toilet paper a little, but the blood was still coming and a few drops splashed on the floor tiles. I pressed the toilet paper back against my nose and moved my foot to cover the red spots on the floor. I leaned back as casually as I could against the sink.

And then out of nowhere, Tracy said, "Hey, we should hang out sometime."

"Sure," I said, in the same muffled voice.

"We don't have to if you don't want to."

"No, that'd be nice."

"You sure?"

"Yeah," I said.

"You really don't have to if you don't want to."

"No, I think that'd be nice."

"You think?"

"Yeah, I—"

"You should get clear, Alex. On what it is you want."

I opened my mouth but didn't say anything.

She laughed and said she was just giving me a hard time.

I felt too slow for her, like I was always a half step behind. I wished I didn't have a wad of toilet paper in front of my face. I wondered if this conversation counted as flirting.

"It's just," I said, and swallowed, "it's just that my nose is still bleeding."

That made her laugh a little, and then I got flustered and turned away from her and hunched over the sink.

"Sorry, sorry," she said, and put her hand on my back. "I didn't mean to laugh. You're just being really adorable."

"It's okay."

I checked to see if the bleeding had stopped and it had, so I took the paper off my face and turned on the faucet. Tracy's hand stayed on my back. I tried to deal with the bits of bloody boogers from just inside my nostrils as best I could and then I had to deal with them on my fingers and then I rinsed my face. I dried off on a towel and turned around to say something, and that's when she asked if she could kiss me.

"Oh," I said. "Sure."

Chapter 3

I woke up before sunrise to the sound of Murphy, our cat, scratching at my door. My eyes cracked open in darkness, and it took a moment for my ears and my brain to arrive at what was happening. Murphy had been doing this lately, waking me up at an ungodly hour. When I was feeling generous, I respected his persistence.

The moment I squeezed toothpaste on my toothbrush and squinted in the bathroom mirror, I remembered that I had been kissed. That's when the day started to crack and settle around me. There was a tingling spot—almost like a touch of peppermint—at the corner of my mouth where the wetness of Tracy's lips had left some wetness on mine. I stood in the bathroom remembering until my eyes were ready to open all the way.

I was Real.

I didn't know it last night. But when Tracy kissed me, that did it. I kissed Tracy. In a cold bathroom. It changed me. I felt the softness of her nose grazing my nose. This morning I could even smell the faintest trace of her on my skin. Her touch had been so soft.

My dad was boiling eggs in the kitchen. He was wearing a red T-shirt and his hair was sticking up. "Good morning good morning," he said.

I poured a bowl of cereal and clicked into my place at the table like a buckle. I felt connected to him. We could be two men in a kitchen. Neither of us was fussy and we both kissed girls.

"What're you guys doing in history class?" he asked.

"The Cold War," I said just because, though we hadn't really done anything yet.

"Ah, yes. That's a really fun one."

And I laughed because I could tell he wanted me to.

On the bus, I relished the sights and sounds that flew past the windows.

At school, I felt a thousand feet tall in the hallway.

I felt a thousand feet tall in front of my locker.

I felt a thousand feet tall waving hello to the people I knew. Jo passed me in the hall, walking quickly while her hands wrangled a bun above her head. She slowed down enough to smile a huge smile and make three quick pats on my shoulder with one of her hands. She even had to regather her hair and start the bun again, all for my sake. That whole morning I didn't rush, I didn't scurry, I just walked. I didn't have to rush for anyone anymore, because I was Real. The world couldn't leave me behind, because I was a part of the world and I was Real.

I was shaky and shy when I said hello to Tracy in English class, but she sat next to me and squeezed my thigh as the bell rang. I didn't pay much attention that period, and then when the bell rang again and we both had to head in separate directions, I didn't know what to say, so I just blurted "Bye!" in a much-too-loud voice. "Bye!" she said, and blushed.

I didn't eat lunch alone. Jen made sure I joined her, Jo, Tracy, and James in their usual spot. The big story of the day was that Jo had had a thing with this other kid in our class over the summer, and he'd sort of stopped talking to her. "He came on really strong," she explained to me, to "catch me up." "We went to the movies a bunch of times. We were hanging out a lot. It was fun. He even met my family at one point, which is a thing."

"For Jo, that's a thing," Jen added.

"But then he ghosted. Like a fade-out . . ."

"Did you talk to him? Did you ask him what happened?" Tracy wanted to know.

"No, not really," Jo said. "And now we're in Spanish class together. It's really awkward. It's like, *Qué hiciste este verano?* And I'm like, *Travis. Yo hice Travis.*" And we all laughed.

"I don't know," she concluded. "I guess we're just going to pretend it never happened." And she shrugged.

"I don't like that," Jen offered, shaking her head, tugging at the paper from her straw. "I feel like that's okay for a week," she said. "But the rest of junior year Spanish is a long time to be pretending." She looked up at Jo. "Why don't you see if you can switch Spanish classes?"

"Noooooo," Jo said, shaking her head. "No no no. It's not that big of a deal."

"It *is* a big deal!" Jen insisted.

Tracy agreed. "It *is* a big deal. But that's not how you're going to handle it. What you're going to do is talk to him. You're going to wait for him after class one day and say, *Hey, we need to talk about this summer.*"

"He's not going to want to talk about it," Jen hedged.

"Maybe not," Tracy insisted. "But it's only fair."

"Things aren't always fair."

"I know. But that's why it's important to try to make them that way."

Jo turned to James. "What do you think, James?" she asked. "As an average meathead?"

A slow smile spread across James's face. It was obviously a long-standing joke between them. People said

James was in love with Jen and that was why he always ate with her and Jo and Tracy. People also said he once kicked his dad out of his house for hitting his mom. All through lunch he kept looking at me with this sly, blank smile but he didn't ever address me. Everyone in the school knew James. People *probably* knew Tracy, as the class genius; they *maybe* knew Jen and Jo. But James was friendly with everyone. He was the kind of boy who made me nervous. He was the kind of boy who made me feel not-Real.

"Speaking as an average meathead," he said, "I think the guy's an asshole."

The laugh that moved through me wasn't a fake laugh, but it took a pathway through my body that my laughs didn't usually take. It startled me. I had a panicked thought of Mabel and wondered where the parts of me that laughed with Mabel would go. Would they leave me? I glanced at my phone, as if a text from her might have an answer. But there wasn't any text.

Tracy's right foot found its way over to mine. We pressed against each other just a little.

I once confessed to Mabel that I thought I was a

tiny bit attracted to guys. When Mabel got excited, I told her to calm down.

"I don't plan on acting on *any* of that *anytime* soon," I said.

"But aren't you ready to fall in love?" Mabel asked.

"Maybe . . . when I'm twenty-five," I replied. But there was something about how serious I sounded when I said it that made us both start laughing. We couldn't stop. I think that was the day we became best friends.

The pressure of Tracy's leg against mine made my body tingle and my heart flutter. Mabel felt very far away. *I guess I like girls, too,* I said to myself. *And I guess I don't have to wait till I'm twenty-five.*

I was a little bit relieved.

The week passed in a flash. By Tuesday I'd put dividers in binders and made labels for the sections. By Wednesday I'd outlined a reading on "Approaches to History" for Ms. Graybill and written a reading response on the novel we read over the summer for Ms. Lewiston. I'd memorized sixteen new verbs for Spanish and diagrammed twenty-some reactions for chemistry. Jake Florieau had taken to giving me high fives when we passed each other in the hallway. Each time I blushed and high-fived him back.

The morning bell sounded the same as it always had, the stairwells had the same sour smell, and all the same teachers waved at me as I passed. But everything was different now that Tracy and I were together. It felt like I could snip ties with the past and let it float away, let go of all the years I wasn't Real. Except for one thing: I missed Mabel. And something was keeping me from telling her about Tracy.

Why? Something about this new life felt like a weird betrayal. Mabel and I had built our friendship on being *in-between* kinds of people, on being *heartbroken and full of longing and frustration and desire*—basically what I considered *not-Real.* But if that was true, how could it be that all of a sudden I was a Real boy dating a Real girl? Mabel had gone from being my other half to being a name in my phone, and whenever I looked up from that little rectangular screen at the people around me, I felt like I was living a double life.

Late Wednesday night Mabel texted me a picture of her new Pittsburgh bedroom. I could see a postcard I'd given her taped above the desk. "How's it going?" she asked. I replied with a heart, a shrug, and an "I miss you"—and that was about it. When I put down the phone, my stomach dropped into my ankles and I swear I almost started to cry.

Thursday at lunch I sat with what was now the usual crew and listened and followed along. I didn't say much. After chemistry, our last class of the day, Tracy and I got our things from our lockers and walked down to the parking lot together, where I would catch my bus. I felt a sudden desire to spend all my free time hanging out with her.

"Would you want to go see a movie or something this weekend?" I asked.

"Sure," she replied, with a little smile. "How about tomorrow?"

I said that sounded great, and she said she'd pick me up.

Chapter 4

On Friday night I opened the car door and got in. We were excited to see each other, and we said so. She put an address in her phone, and a voice told her to head north on Old York Road. She put on some music and a man was singing, asking a woman to *stay, stay, please don't go.*

For a while we didn't know what to say to each other. Or maybe I just didn't know what to say to her.

"How're you liking being back?" I offered.

"I like it," she replied. "I mean, it's what we do,

right? School? It's nice to have a break, but I was getting ready to get back to it."

"Yeah," I said sympathetically. "I'll be excited when it's all over with, though."

"Really? You don't like school?"

"Not particularly."

"Huh," Tracy said. "You're good at it, though. There must be some part of you that likes it."

"I don't hate it. I'm just getting through it, I guess."

"To what?"

"Sorry?"

"Getting through it to what? What is it you're so excited about on the other side of all this school?"

I'd never considered the question before.

"Oh," I said. "I don't know. I guess just . . . real life? Like being a person in the world."

"This is real life. You're a person, this is the world. As far as I can tell."

"I know, but . . ."

"But what?" Tracy asked.

"Maybe I don't feel particularly real yet," I said. "Like this world is just something I have to move through until I can get to a place where I can be a real person. I know it doesn't make a whole lot of sense."

"But what do you even do, then? If that's how you feel? Like, what do you do in your free time? Is that a weird question?"

"I don't know," I said. "I like to play with our cat. I like to read. I like documentaries."

At a red light she reached over and pinched me in the stomach.

"Ow!"

The light turned green.

"What was that for?"

"You said you felt like you weren't a real person," she said, and bit the tip of her tongue between her teeth in the most charming way. "I wanted to test and see."

At the movie theater, I bought our tickets with my mom's credit card ("My turn next time," Tracy said), and we skipped buying popcorn because Tracy had a bag of it and two cans of soda in her purse. She said, "Hey, Derek!" to the guy taking tickets and stuck out her tongue. He said something I couldn't hear, and Tracy laughed.

As we settled into our big red seats, I wanted to tell her never mind and that I thought she had a point about being real, but the previews had started and she said, "Shhh!" and tapped my knee. "I want to watch these." Then she turned and landed a kiss just in front of my ear.

Afterward we made out in her car. Now it was like *I* was in a movie. At first I felt a bunch of pressure to do a good job, but then it seemed like it was going okay without having to worry about it too much. I figured I'd just say something if I felt weird. I could always pretend that I had to sneeze or something. Our mouths started to open a little bit. I felt the nub of her tongue testing for mine. It made me think of a pencil eraser. Her nose was cold and her tongue was cold from the ice in her soda, but the rest of her mouth was hot. I could taste the sweetness of the Coke and the salt of the popcorn. There was a tap on the window. It was a security guard. We separated and said, *Sorry* and looked at our laps.

My body tingled where Tracy had touched me.

I looked out the passenger window. Everyone had gone home. The lot was empty. The mall was dark. The sky was huge. The security guard looked tired, and her flashlight seemed heavy. She watched us buckle our seat belts and then she walked away.

We turned on the car and the clock lit up. It was after eleven. It felt like we were the only two living creatures in a dead and silent world. I started to pretend that I didn't care about curfew, but then I realized Tracy cared about curfew, too, so I said, *Yeah, we should probably get back.* She raced uptown so we could both make it home in time, and the whole way we were shivering and laughing and barely able to talk. I couldn't stop giggling. I watched my fingers wiggle like little creatures in my lap.

"I don't usually get in trouble," I said to her. "Is that a weird thing to say?"

"No," she said. "I don't usually get in trouble either."

"Did we just get in trouble?" I asked, tucking anxiety under something that seemed like flirting.

"No," she said with a nervous chuckle. "I don't think so. But I know what you mean."

I have very few memories of my parents getting mad at me. I can picture my dad yelling when I was nine years old: there was a play I wanted to see, a version of *Cinderella* this children's theater was doing, and he told me we couldn't go, because my cousins were visiting and the weekend was too busy blah blah blah. But even after that I kept thinking about the play, and something in me started to ache and wouldn't stop aching and I decided to ask one more time.

"Could we just—"

"Will you drop that stupid play already, Alex?" he shouted. "It is absolutely not on the table!"

And my face got hot and I felt ashamed of myself. "It's not a stupid play!" I shouted back, and went up to my room. I sat crying in my room, staring at the poster image of Cinderella and her stepsisters in their ball gowns.

Tracy switched off the car in front of my house. She turned to me.

"Hey, do we want to do this? Do we want to like do this as a thing?"

I looked at her dark, flushed skin right then, at the way her hair swooped behind her ear and ended in a point at the back of her neck. I hadn't realized it *wasn't* a thing. It had already changed my life.

"Do we want to do this?" she asked again, and I realized that I'd just been staring, marveling. It seemed like every sadness I'd ever felt was behind me now, like sadness would be impossible from here on out. And this new voice of mine spoke, in a late-night bloom of joy:

"Yeah," I said.

And I started to grin.

"Yeah," I said again. "I think we do."

Chapter 5

Once we were back in school, word got out quickly. Tuesday morning in English class I heard Lorie Guzman say our names in one breath, TracyandAlex. Jayson Williams came up to me after history class on Wednesday to ask if "you guys," meaning me and Tracy, were going on the Spanish trip this year. On Thursday, Mr. Wolper-Diaz, who everyone knows keeps track of which students are dating, made it official: he smiled faintly when we picked each other as lab partners and put a little mark in his book. We sat together in all the classes we shared, and we talked as we walked together in the halls.

I decided that if I was really going to do this thing with Tracy, I should probably take her to some of the places Mabel and I used to go. Not that I needed things between me and Tracy to be like they were between me and Mabel. But I wanted to *bring something to the table*, if that makes sense.

Carma's didn't feel right, because that was just a coffee shop. But there was this place—the Lavender Ladder, it was called—where I'd gone with Mabel a couple of times to see bands. It had been a furniture store back in the seventies, and my dad says he remembers going there with his mom once to pick out a dresser. It was boarded up for a long time, but then a bunch of people turned it into an arts center and DIY venue and gallery kind of place. Most Tuesday nights Mabel went to a queer teen group they had. They were having a queer film festival, and I figured I could take Tracy.

"Wait, so what's it called again?" she asked, when I told her my idea for our next date.

"The Lavender Ladder."

"And it's in Baltimore?"

"Down by Patterson Park."

"How have I never heard of this place?"

I shrugged and said I wasn't sure.

"And what's happening there?"

"It's this queer film festival," I said, watching Tracy's face for any flicker of a reaction.

"And what's showing Friday?"

"Friday it's this movie *Querelle*. I don't know much about it, but I hear it's kind of a classic."

Tracy studied me a moment. "You think I'm a really serious person, don't you?"

I frowned a little.

"But I actually think," she said, "that you're maybe a little bit more serious than I am." And then she kissed me. "Don't worry," she added. "I'm excited."

I drove us in my dad's car through warm dusky light past the cemetery and the new hospital buildings with pedestrian walkways over the street. After a stretch of treeless blocks filled with barbershops and takeout places, we were under trees again and the low sun flashed in the front windows as we passed. Tracy was describing her life plan. She told me she would leave Baltimore for college and go straight from college to law school, ideally at Yale or Columbia. After a year or two of working for a judge somewhere, maybe New York or DC, she'd come back to Baltimore and get involved in city government. She wanted to live in Mount Vernon or Bolton Hill. As she spoke, I thought about how little time I'd spent imagining my own future.

We passed the park. The sunlight on the buildings had thickened to butter-gold. I had the window down and you could hear kids laughing and shouting and a set of speakers pouring out hip-hop. The air had its hand on my face. I'd learned my way around Baltimore with Mabel, but here, now, bringing someone new to a place she'd never heard of, I felt closer to this city than I ever had.

Tracy asked me if I thought I'd always live in Baltimore. The word *always* snapped me out of whatever private moment I was having, and I said I wasn't sure.

She asked what my gut told me. I said I'd always liked the sound of California. Tracy nodded and said it was important to her to give back to the place that made her who she was.

"But if you want to run away," she said, "good riddance."

And then she laughed.

My heart jumped. I was trying to think of a funny way to answer her, but then there was a parking spot and I had to grab it.

The Lavender Ladder was smaller than I remembered. The front room was a low-ceilinged rectangle with spotlights mounted on tracks on the ceiling, and there was a gallery show on the walls. The floors were scuffed linoleum, and there were stacks of folding chairs leaning against the wall. I bought us tickets from someone with big plastic earrings that stretched holes in their ears. The screening was through a door, in what I think had been storage. We found seats toward the front. I was nervous and talkative.

"Mabel used to come here a lot. She brought me to see bands a few times, and I always liked it." I looked around. I wanted to be able to say something else about the place, but I didn't know much more than that. "There's a youth group that meets on Tuesday nights."

"How long have you and Mabel known each other?"

"Just since freshman year."

"Funny," she said. "I would have figured you'd grown up together. You always seemed like you were scheming stuff. Maybe this is weird to say, but Jen used to call the two of you the Pirates."

I blushed and was also maybe a little proud of that. "We just hung out a lot, I guess." I was staring at the *Filthy Classix of Queer Cinema* program in my hand and maybe starting to regret my choice of a second date. "How about you? How long have you and Jen and Jo all known each other?"

"We went to the same middle school. Jen and Jo have been good friends since they were really little. And then the three of us started hanging out in like seventh grade."

"Oh, so you go back a ways . . ."

I was going to ask Tracy what she'd been like as a kid, but someone went up to the mic and started making announcements: "Turn off your phones please, everyone. Exit the way you came in. There's free pop-corn in the back . . ." Then the lights went down. I wished I'd gotten us popcorn. It seemed too late now; I didn't want to make the other people in our row get up.

The movie started—music and the first of the cred-its. I could tell almost immediately that it was going to be *a lot*. And I wasn't sure if Tracy would like it. The story, if you could call it that, was about a bunch of sailors who all wanted to have sex with each other. They were simultaneously very repressed and very horny. The narrator kept saying cryptic things about desire. At one point I heard Tracy sigh and fold her program in half with a sharp crease down the mid-dle. The main character, Querelle, tried to seduce someone, couldn't, and then slit the person's throat. At the same time, all the older men were in love with Querelle. The acting was weird and stiff and it looked like someone had painted all the backdrops in poster paint. There were literally giant stone penises built into the pier where the sailors hung out. I could feel the tension growing in Tracy's body. She was either really uncomfortable or she hated it.

Everyone else in the room seemed to be having a great time. Someone honked with laughter like a truck backing up and someone hissed *Shhhhhhhhhhhh!* Querelle and his brother got into a fistfight and the man to my left with lime-green fingernails grabbed my arm and shouted, "Baby!" That made me laugh, but Tracy's silence shut me down again. I was frustrated because I just wanted her to have a good time and I felt like she would if she just lightened up.

Something weird was starting to dawn on me. I was here on a date with Tracy, but I felt more connected to everyone else in the room—people I didn't know— than to the person sitting beside me, the person who was apparently my girlfriend. When I thought about it that way, I started to get angry. I wanted to shake Tracy and say, *They're all having a great time. Why can't we have a great time with them?* I remembered that a few times now Tracy had pinched me or poked me like I was a weird little animal. I hated that. *I actually think that you're maybe a little bit more serious than I am.* Why? Just because I was excited about an old movie?

She didn't get me. I was an *in-between* kind of person after all.

It ended and the lights came on. The floor was littered with popcorn, and the recycling bins were rapidly filling with seltzer and ginger ale cans.

"All right," Tracy said, almost under her breath, and touched my wrist. "I'm gonna go use the bathroom."

"Okay," I answered.

I was grinding my teeth.

Then I noticed someone by the popcorn machine. Or, I heard him before I saw him: he was laughing a high, giddy laugh. The laugh was coming out of a tall, skinny body with a round face and a shock of blue hair. He was telling a story to someone I couldn't see, shaking his hands like he was shaking someone's shoulders. He was curved, like a parenthesis, and he had on a short green T-shirt. Maybe my age, but confident.

He finished what he was saying and looked over my way. His face was open and expressive, like a child's. His eyes met mine, and I saw a flicker of surprise—or interest?—as his mouth twitched into a smile. I managed to lift the corners of my lips in response.

"You ready to go?" Tracy was there at my elbow.

"Sure," I said.

We didn't talk much in the car.

It was 12:03 when I got back. My dad was asleep. My mom was in her pajamas, putting things away in the kitchen. She asked how the movie was, and didn't seem to notice that I was three minutes past curfew. I said it was good. She yawned and nodded and kissed me good night.

Tracy called as I was about to brush my teeth.

"Just wanted to say good night," she said. "And sorry for being such a grouch on the way home. I think that whole movie just put me in a mood."

"Oh, it's all good," I said, keeping my voice steady. A moment passed. "Is everything okay?"

"Yeah, I just . . . it was weird watching that movie with you. For a while I thought you had an agenda.

Like, why would Alex take me to this movie? What is he trying to tell me? It almost felt a little aggressive."

"Oh," I said quietly. "No . . ."

"And that made me kind of angry. But then I realized I was overthinking it. And you probably didn't know much about it and thought it might be good. And then I felt less angry. And I felt bad for being so grumpy about it all."

It was such a relief, hearing her say that, that all the good feelings I had about her came flooding back. "It's okay," I said.

"Am I right, then? Did you know anything about that movie going in?"

"No, I just thought it might be interesting."

"Great. Wonderful," she said. "I'm glad my suspicions were correct."

The moment hung there between us.

"I had a really nice time hanging out with you, Tracy," I told her. And it felt true, even if it meant forgetting how angry I'd been during the movie.

"Me too, Alex. Let's do it again?"

"Definitely."

Chapter 6

"So how was your date last night?" my dad wanted to know, once I'd made it downstairs. It was Saturday morning, and he was making omelets. I woke up to the rattle of pan against burner; I smelled garlic and onion. Now I was in the kitchen, and there were bowls and spoons and cutting boards everywhere. "Was this the same girl as last time? What was her name? How did it go?"

"It was fine," I said.

"What's her name?" my mom asked.

"Tracy."

"Tracy. Tracy." My mom was the one with the good memory. "Do we know her?"

"I don't know. I don't think so. I don't think you've met her."

"Do you guys have a lot of classes together?"

"Um, some. We've got English together, and chemistry, and—"

"Is that how you met her?"

"No, we sort of knew each other before. We—"

"You like her?" my dad cut in.

"Yeah," I replied. "I do."

"Your first girlfriend, huh?" he added with a smile.

"I don't know . . ."

"A part of me always thought you and Mabel would end up—"

"*Peter.*"

I had told my dad a thousand times that Mabel dated girls. But somehow it never stuck.

"No, and I love Mabel," he said. "But this is great, too."

"I just remembered." My mom put her book and

coffee down and started upstairs. "I got you these shirts."

While she was getting the shirts, my dad gave me his advice. "Just go slow," he said. He was scooping eggs and cheese and mushrooms onto a plate. "I know it's all very exciting, and you're going to want to rush into things, but that never ends well. I remember when I was your age—"

"Here, honey, I got this gray and this blue. Will you try them on and let me know what you think?"

"Let the kid eat," my dad said.

"Of course, Peter, just—for later."

"You like those eggs?"

"Yeah," I said. "They're good."

My mom held each shirt up in turn. They were heavy cotton button-downs, one with stripes and one with a simple pattern.

She held one up for me. "Will you at least tell me if you like them?"

"Sure," I said, with a glance, sighing in my head. "I like them."

I always felt wrong in baggy button-downs like that, like I was walking around wrapped in big sheets of foam. But whenever my mom was at the mall, she'd buy a few on sale and bring them home. I felt too guilty to object, especially since there wasn't anything I could say I'd rather wear. Having a mom who buys you clothes is a nice thing, right? Sometimes, though, I felt like a small dog my mom dressed up and sent out into the world.

She was still holding up the shirts, waiting for me to take a proper look. "I think they're nice, sweetie . . ."

Flickers of anger started to rise from my stomach and tease at my shoulders. It was similar to the anxious anger I'd swallowed the night before with Tracy. What the hell was upsetting me?

"Yeah," I said, "I agree. Thank you."

Why was I being so stupid about this? If I didn't want the dumb shirts, what did I want instead? When I asked myself that question, my brain short-circuited somehow and all the sparks and smoke turned me around and sent me back to where I'd come from, which was nowhere.

Meanwhile my dad was doing his *guys are just guys* thing. My dad isn't like a dude-bro or anything, but he loves shaking my shoulder and talking about *guys like us.*

"He doesn't care about the shirts," he was saying. "He cares about his new girlfriend."

"Oh . . . ," I started to say.

"I'd say that most guys care more about girls than they do about clothes. Wouldn't you agree?"

I was ready to smash my plate and crawl under the house. Maybe my life just wasn't mine. Maybe it belonged to them. It felt like my life would never actually be mine. My parents would keep tracking it and thinking about it and telling me what it was all about until I got old and they were even older and one of us died.

I took a deep breath. I don't think they had any idea I was feeling what I was feeling. My mom rolled her eyes ever so slightly and folded the shirts. My dad came around behind me and dropped his hands on my shoulders and gave me an affectionate shake.

"Our son, our son!" he said, with pride in his voice. "He's growing up."

The morning stretched into afternoon. It was a typical Saturday in our house. Dishes in the sink, the back door open; outside, someone raking, kids playing. Once the anger passed, I messed around on my phone for a while, watching trailers for the kinds of documentaries I liked but knew would never play in Baltimore, and then I settled down with my homework. My mom went out to do errands while my dad caught up on emails.

Tracy texted me a picture of a backyard, filled with people. She was at her uncle's birthday party.

"I keep thinking about you," she texted.

"Me too," I texted back.

Every once in a while, my chest got tight with a twitch of the confusing, free-floating anger I'd felt the night before, during *Querelle*. Then I'd shake it off and go back to focusing on homework. And every once in a while, I thought of the boy with the blue hair.

Chapter 7

The next afternoon, after homework, Tracy and I met up in the park by Lake Roland. The birds were noisy in the last hour of sunlight, and we walked up the path away from the parking lot. Tracy said she'd been describing me to her mom.

"What did you tell her about me?"

"Oh, I don't know. I told her you were really smart and funny and attractive and that I liked you a lot."

"You flatter me."

"I mean it. Maybe this is weird to say," she said,

"but I haven't done a lot of this before. Like, going on real dates with anybody."

"Yeah," I said. "Me neither."

"Well I like it. I like how easy it is with you."

I didn't answer. I just took her hand in mine and squeezed it, and then we swung our arms together in a big swooping arc. A pair of dogs ran up to us and nudged our crotches, and their owner called for them and apologized and called for them again and they went bounding off into the dusk. Then Tracy pointed up and I caught a last look at a flock of birds in silhouette, twisting and diving, before they disappeared behind the tree line. Already a cold, wet mist hung over the grass, and there was the littlest pinch in the air that made me think ahead to winter.

We continued up the hill. I put my arm around Tracy and felt her warmth. We paused at a picnic table. I sat on one of the benches and she sat on the tabletop, facing me, her legs on either side of my legs, and she took my face in her hands and kissed me.

In moments like this, everything felt easy and right. *This* was what I wanted. *This* was the way I wanted to be. But then I'd see my own hands, which seemed too big on her slender arms, and I'd wish I could send my body away and just be touch, and lips, and the flutter of a heartbeat.

Then we were both lying on our backs on the table, looking up at the sky. The moon was big and you could start to see the stars. Tracy proposed that we make this our special spot, and I said I liked that idea. I slid over a few inches and pressed the side of my body against the side of hers.

It wasn't until her mom called to ask where she was that we started back toward the parking lot.

At lunch, we talked about whether Mr. Alstead and Mrs. Young were having an affair and whether our school could be considered "diverse" if the Latinx kids in each grade mostly hung out with Latinx kids and the handful of white kids basically stuck together. On the rare occasions when I made a comment, James looked at me and nodded, which I took to mean he liked me a lot. Jo asked our advice about whether it was weird to invite the senior she had a crush on to go with her while she got her hair cut.

That Thursday I was supposed to go over to Tracy's house for dinner.

I stood in my room and picked up one of the shirts my mom had gotten me—the gray one, with dusty blue stripes. Why had I gotten so worked up about these stupid shirts? If my dad was right, I wasn't supposed to care about clothes. I shoved my anxiety down in a dark corner of my brain, shut the door on it, and put on the shirt.

I was probably just nervous about meeting Tracy's parents.

Her mom was named Jennifer; she was friendly and had made vegetable lasagna. Tracy showed me her room and seemed very glad when I said I liked it. There was a small yellow couch in the corner, covered in stuffed animals. I imagined Tracy's hands rearranging the bears and the dogs and the rabbits, smoothing the brown comforter on her bed, and straightening the orange pillows. Above the couch there was a postcard-size photograph of Toni Morrison, and on her desk were framed pictures of Jo and Jen and James and a few other people I didn't know. Tracy introduced her dad, just home from work in impeccably pressed pants, who greeted me with a strong, enveloping handshake and asked if I would describe myself as a sports fan. ("*Dad*," Tracy said to that.) Tracy's kid brother, Antony, shook my hand, too, and did a little dance in his white socks. We sat and served ourselves and talked about the people running for mayor. We talked about Antony's school project on dinosaurs.

Whenever I meet new grown-ups, it's like a wheel starts whirring very fast in my head. And the wheel is powering the light in my eyes and the smile on my face. And I get a little bumbly but also pretty charming, I think. And the wheel is spinning the whole time, trying to make sure I laugh the right amount and say good things and act polite but not too formal. I want to show that I am thoughtful but not pretentious, warm but not goofy. All through dinner I was focused on that.

"You two are both so lucky," Tracy's mom was saying.

"You know that? Don't ever take it for granted. You go to a good school, you have nice families, you have so much. You can't ever take that for granted—"

"You know what I wouldn't take for granted?" Antony asked. "The new *Dragon Ball Z* for PS4."

"All right, Antony," his mom said, and we all laughed.

When I got home I was exhausted.

I ran up to my room, flopped on my bed, and pulled out my phone. Mabel had sent a picture. When I saw it, my chest cracked open and my insides spilled out. For a second I couldn't breathe. It was the two of us, sophomore year, standing in her bedroom. I hadn't realized that picture still existed. I wished I could teleport back to that moment; I wished I could be with Mabel again, laughing, in that house. I took a deep breath and used my fingers to zoom in on each of us and I squinted, holding the phone close to my face.

Mabel's aunt Agatha had visited for Christmas. Agatha was a tarot reader and a painter and worked sometimes in an office, sometimes in a quilting store, in

Wise, Virginia. I'd met her once before, and I was over at Mabel's when she arrived Christmas Eve morning. She pulled up in front of Mabel's house in her beat-up, dusty blue Nissan Versa and emptied the trunk of six or seven bags of clothes.

"These are for my beautiful queer niece. Take what you like and bring the rest to the Goodwill. I won't be offended, because I won't know," she said, and winked.

Three days later, after Agatha left, I was sprawled on Mabel's bed while she dug through the clothes.

"Does this make me look like a motorcycle dyke?" she asked, swiveling her hips in a dark blue jumpsuit with a red stripe up the side.

Or, wearing a little veiled hat whose name we had to look up (a "fascinator"), she'd perch on the edge of the bed: "My dahhhling. I've been bereft since the funeral. Simply bereft."

"Who *is* this person?" I asked at one point, meaning Agatha, as I picked up a pair of cowboy boots, and marveled at the nonsensical-seeming mixture of looks.

"Oh, you know." Mabel grinned. "Just a witchy

lesbian of a certain age who doesn't like to be pinned down."

"Can I try some on?" I asked.

"By all means."

We spent probably two hours putting on and taking off shirts, shoes, dresses, skirts, and hats. Agatha's bags seemed endless. Everything smelled like dust and lavender. We talked to each other in stupid voices and gave ourselves name after made-up name. It was only after we'd found the outfits that seemed too right to ever want to take off that we decided to record the moment. Now, almost nine months later, in my bedroom, I squinted at the image of Mabel in a tuxedo with sleeves too short for her long arms. A razor-thin mustache in eyeliner pencil completed the look. She had announced in a gravelly voice that her name was "Jimmy Crevasse."

I slid the zoomed image over and squinted at the person standing beside her, with a hand draped over the nearby bedpost: me. I had on a green velvet dress that fell to just below my knees. There had been plenty of pants and cowboy shirts in the bag, but none of them seemed exciting to try on. The dress was calling me, even though I'd never worn a dress before. There was a little bit of trim around the neck, which opened in a rectangle around my collarbone. I had a string of blue plastic diamonds around my neck. I could still remember how exciting it felt to wear that dress, and how dangerous.

"And who do we have here, little lady?" Mabel had asked me, a moment before we took the picture.

"Who, me?" I said, playing for time, since I wanted a name as good as Jimmy Crevasse. I felt a bit silly. And I also felt like a Russian aristocrat. "Me?" I said again. "You may call me Sasha." But that didn't seem good enough, since Sasha could be a boy's name or a girl's name. I wanted something striking, something complete. So I said it again, with an addition. "You may call me Sasha Masha." And I offered the back of my hand for Jimmy Crevasse to kiss.

Which, like a gentleman, he did.

Lying on my bed, looking at our faces in the photograph from what felt like a different life, I thought we looked young. We were kids. But there was something else in our eyes that struck me now. We were looking at the camera with a calm, thousand-yard stare. It was as if somewhere inside of us we knew everything already—everything we'd ever need to know. I wondered what I'd since forgotten.

I went downstairs to get a snack, thinking I should call Mabel. Probably it was time to tell her I'd started dating Tracy, tell her I'd become a Real Boy and hope that she didn't feel betrayed. I was growing up. I wasn't the kid in that photograph anymore. Probably Mabel was growing up, too, in ways I didn't know yet. She'd understand.

In the kitchen my mom was eating a cut-up apple, paging through the circular that came every week with coupons from the drugstore.

"Hi, sweetie," she said. "You deep in homework?"

"Yeah," I said. "I've got to outline this history section." I'd already given my mom a report on how dinner went, if by *report* I mean a series of short, general answers to an endless stream of questions. *Yes, they were nice, yes, I had a good time, yes, the food was good, yes, their house was pretty, yes yes yes.* I peered into the cabinet to consider my snack options.

"Are you feeling okay? You seem a little out of it."

"Yeah," I said. "I'm just tired and have a lot of studying to do."

"They work you very hard."

"It's all right."

"Are you finding good people to hang out with at school? Besides Tracy, I mean. I know it must be hard without Mabel."

"Yeah, it's good, I hang out with people. They're mostly friends of Tracy's."

"Did you know them before, or . . . ?"

"I sort of knew them. But not super well."

"And how's Ms. Wilson? I know Ms. Garcia was so great, it's a hard act to follow."

"No, she's good, I like her."

I pulled down a bag of pita chips and poured some into a bowl.

"I worry about you sometimes, sweetie," my mom said, after a moment. "You seem like you've been stressed out a little bit."

What was with all the questions? I was tired, and I had too much reading to do. Couldn't I just get a snack and go do my homework in peace?

"I'm fine, Mom, really," I said. I put on my best, sunniest, most likable smile and went back upstairs.

Murphy was waiting for me on my bed. Dear Murphy. That day Mabel and I went through Agatha's clothes, I'd brought home this windbreaker and a pair of jeans that fit me. Murphy came up to them and sniffed them a while, then turned and settled in with his back nestled against them. The smell of those clothes—the gust of a new reality they'd brought into Mabel's and my day—didn't concern Murphy any longer than the few moments he needed to take it in. It was funny to remember how easily Murphy could adjust to a new reality.

"You wanna take the dress? The Sasha Masha

dress?" Mabel had asked me as I was leaving. "It suits you."

"Nah," I said, though I had a knot in my belly. "When am I ever going to wear it?"

It was getting late. I'd have to call Mabel tomorrow. I started back in on my history outline, wishing people could be more like cats. Sniff, settle in, move on.

Chapter 8

"Can I tell you something weird, Maybelline?"

"Of course, Alexidore."

"I think I'm dating Tracy Lewis."

There was a pause.

"You think?"

I coughed. "I'm dating Tracy Lewis."

There was another pause.

"Well, congrats, babe! Cupid strikes again."

"Maybe," I said, blushing and relieved. "We'll see."

That was easier than I thought.

"Sounds like you're taking over the school," she said. "All according to plan."

I laughed. I was suddenly full of things I wanted to say. I tried to describe *Querelle* and struggled to remember what the officer-narrator had said about humility . . . or humiliation . . . I did my best serious art-film voice. Soon we were giggling like we were back in one of our bedrooms, lying on the floor on a random Thursday night. Then I asked her about her dating life, and she groaned and said she was sure she'd die alone.

"The life of a dyke in Pittsburgh," she said. "Amiright?"

"Surely you're not the only dyke in Pittsburgh!"

"No . . . ," she admitted.

Soon we were laughing again.

"All right, Alexidore," Mabel said with a contented sigh. "I think I've gotta go."

My heart felt very full. I wondered if the wall between life with Mabel and life with Tracy would start to crumble now—now that I'd explained myself.

"I'll talk to you soon," she said.

"Bye, Maybelline," I replied. "Miss you."

Things with Tracy started to move pretty quickly.

The week after I went over to her house for dinner, Tracy came over to mine. She wore a cream-colored sweater and looked beautiful. I put on my other nice new shirt and sat up straight. My dad wanted to tell all these old stories about me, things I'd heard him tell a thousand times. Tracy was eating them up, but I wanted to crawl out of my skin. As soon as she left, my dad came up to me and clapped me on the shoulder and gave me an affectionate shake.

We had another Friday-night date, this time Vietnamese food. And then that Sunday I spent the whole day over at her house. It rained and rained. We sat on the yellow couch and watched eighties music videos on YouTube. Antony showed us the turnip seedlings he was growing for his science project. Around dusk the rain slowed, and Tracy gave me a ride home. The house was empty. I stretched out on my bed and could smell Tracy on my clothes.

Pretty soon light jackets became heavy jackets. All the trees in the neighborhood looked like they were on fire. It had been a month since Tracy kissed me in Jen's bathroom.

I liked the feeling I got when I was close to Tracy. But it was weird: whenever I happened to see what we looked like together—in a store window, the mirror in the hall, wherever—I'd feel oafish and clumsy and wrong. It was the thing I'd felt when I saw my big hands on her thin arms: that these hands weren't right, somehow. I'd have moments when I felt that about my whole body. It was too big, too bulky. It was . . . *what, exactly?*

Wrong was really the only word. This was worse than being not-Real. It was Real in the wrong direction.

One Saturday the debate team was set to compete as part of a tournament out in the suburbs. I woke up at six and drove with Tracy as spectator and supporter. In the car she practiced her arguments for and against voting rights for people with felonies on their record, and I asked questions. The sun was just coming up as we parked. Subdued voices echoed in the unfamiliar school lobby and the air smelled like coffee; we stood for a moment in a circle with the other debate kids from our school, all in nice clothes and name tags, and then Tracy and I were speed-walking down a hallway toward the first of her matches. It was a round-robin competition among five different schools. Over the course of the day, Tracy faced off against a series of other debaters—all boys, all white—and destroyed them all.

"Not bad, huh?" she asked me, after we'd said goodbye to the rest of the team and started walking out to her car.

"That was pretty cool," I said, feeling very proud of my girlfriend. "You were the only girl—the only Black girl—the only Black debater."

"Oh, I'm aware," she said with a wink. "I'm always aware."

It struck me that I spent a lot of my life trying not to stick out. On an afternoon like today, in a place like this debate tournament, Tracy had no choice.

"How . . . ," I started to say, not sure what I was trying to ask. "How does that feel? To stand out like that? Is that a weird thing to ask?"

Tracy shook her head. "I feel really alive when I debate. It's maybe why I like it so much. And being different," she said, cocking her head a little, "that feels like life. I just try to own it." She buckled her seat belt. "Wanna get some food?"

Mabel generally thought schoolwork was overrated and rolled her eyes at me when I showed that I cared. So I was too embarrassed to tell her that for our first English assignment, Tracy and I swapped papers. I'd decided I wanted to up my game. I wrote comments on her essay and she wrote comments on mine. Her writing was clear and strong; mine felt wobbly and vague in comparison. But she showed me some things I could cut, and the paper got better.

Our next assignment, though, came on a day when I was in one of my irritable moods. It was a history reading response, and that night Tracy texted to propose a deadline for us to send drafts to each other. I texted that I didn't think I wanted to; I just wanted to do it myself and get it done. She texted to ask if I didn't like her feedback. I texted that I did but that I didn't want to always share everything. She texted to ask if I was mad at her. The whole conversation *was* making me mad—I could feel that anger bubbling in my stomach—but I texted back no, with an exclamation point, and promised we could swap on our next one. After that we both stopped texting and I did the rest of my homework. Anyway, by the next day she seemed like she'd forgotten about it, and then it was Friday and Fridays were our nights. We went to hear a singer and a pianist play old songs in the back of a music store.

We had those tense moments every once in a while, moments where we'd get annoyed at each other. I'd get angry and wouldn't say anything about it; I'd just want to be left alone. Then the next day the tension would be gone. Or that's how it seemed.

Mabel and I caught up on the phone every week. I'd walk out into the yard while we were talking and make circles in the grass, kicking my sneakers through the growing piles of fallen leaves. Everything would be flat and yellow in the light from the streetlamps. Mabel said there was a girl she maybe had a crush on.

"What's her name?" I asked.

"Alice," she told me. "Alice Starr."

She sounded small and far away, a voice in my ear.

The following Friday night Tracy and I were hanging out in my room. We'd just come back from getting ramen. I leaned against my pillows, and she sat there on the edge of the bed, looking at me.

"Do you still like doing what we're doing?" she asked, out of the blue. "Do you still want to be dating me?"

I sat up and looked her in the eye. I wasn't used to seeing her so uncertain—insecure, almost. Her eyes were full of worry.

"I do!" I said, and swallowed a startled laugh. "Of course I do! Why are you asking?"

"I don't know," she said. "You've seemed a little weird lately. Like, a little angry."

"I'm not angry," I said, and sighed. "I'm probably just tired."

I lay back, shuffled over toward the wall, and invited

her to lie down beside me. She did, and I wrapped my arms around her. I pressed my nose into her hair and breathed in. Her hand was resting lightly on my shoulder, and she hooked an ankle over mine. She asked me to promise that I'd tell her if I started to have a crush on someone else. I told her of course I would.

"I like you, Tracy. I promise."

"That's a weird thing to promise."

I didn't say anything to that, but eventually her breath slowed down and mine did, too, and our breaths and heartbeat fell into something like a rhythm.

It was almost Halloween.

No matter the cold, at least once a week Tracy and I would lie together in the hammock in her backyard. I'd entwine my legs with hers and we'd talk and not talk and look up at the sky. We'd watch the leaves fall down from the big maple tree above us. We were like two pieces of rope that had been frequently knotted; even when we were separate, our bodies held the shape of the knot we made together.

Chapter 9

~~~~~~~~

Tracy said that real couples had nicknames for each other, so she decided to call me "Mister Alexi." "Is that okay?" she asked, with a teasing half smile. At first I shrugged and said, "Sure, of course." But mostly it made me think of my other name, Sasha Masha. That made my chest squeeze and my throat throb, like my body wanted to cry but my eyes wouldn't.

I told myself it was because I missed my friend. That was all. But one day, the week before Halloween, after a phone call with Mabel that had me very full of the joy of talking with my friend, I still felt down and lost. I could only think of that picture, and I started to wonder whether I really just missed myself.

You miss yourself? How can you miss yourself? You're right here.

I was lying on my bed, trying to think through the feeling.

I missed the person I used to be. The person I was when I was with Mabel.

Who was that person, though? Was that person really all that different from who you are now?

Things felt freer with Mabel, things felt sillier. I felt more alive.

I rolled onto my side and stared at the blue carpet on my floor.

Okay, but let's be honest: Mabel was the one who seemed alive. She was the silly one, she was the fearless one. You were the quiet, smiling, hardworking, compliant, friendly, likable, nice, good kid who tagged along with her and laughed at her jokes. If this was a movie, you were the side-kick. You were the boring one. You say you miss your old self, but what old self was that? You never had an old self. You never had a self the way Mabel had a self. You just followed other people around and enjoyed the ride.

I sat up.

In all the fairy tales, there's always a dream. A voice, a castle, a prince. What was my dream? I hadn't even been able to tell Tracy what I wanted to do after high school. What did I know about myself? What did I want?

When I closed my eyes, all I saw was that velvet dress, and the only words I thought of were: Sasha Masha. *Sasha Masha.* It was a feeling in my body, a look in my eye, maybe the texture of the velvet and the lavender smell from Agatha's trunk. I couldn't figure out much else about it.

What kind of a dream was that?

I was already feeling weird and sad when I came downstairs. My mom was in the kitchen.

"How was your day, sweetie?" she asked.

"It was all right."

"You had Ms. Lewiston today?"

"Yeah, I have her every day."

"What are you guys reading?"

"I already told you."

I was being obnoxious, I knew. But when my mom thought I was upset about something, she would just start asking a lot of questions. And the more questions she asked, the more upset I got, and the more upset I got, the more determined she was to figure out what was upsetting me, and the more she tried to figure it out, the more determined I was to get her to stop.

"You seem upset, sweetie," she finally said.

Then something snapped inside of me, and I turned and faced her and roared, "I JUST WANT PEOPLE TO LEAVE ME ALONE, OKAY!!"

It sounded mean and stupid leaving my mouth, even I knew that, the way my voice cracked like a little kid's, but in a haze of frustration and shame, I ran upstairs and slammed the door.

I needed to get out of here. Where could I go? I didn't want to go to Tracy's, and Mabel didn't live here. What other actual friends did I have? Then I had an idea. What about the Lavender Ladder? What if they were doing another screening? I could watch a movie and be by myself.

On their website it said no movie. But tonight was Queer Talk for Teens, and that was Mabel's old group. There would be people there. It was somewhere to be.

Why not?

I put on my shoes.

"I'm going to the movies!" I shouted, and didn't wait for an answer.

"I think we're going to get started," someone said in a loud voice, and the fifteen or twenty people in the room began to find their way to chairs. These were all young people, a different crowd than had been at the screening. They could have been high-school age, they could have been older. I couldn't tell. I stood in the doorway.

"Hey, boo!" The person who'd spoken was looking at me. "Come on in. You can shut the door behind you."

I shut the door and moved toward the ring of chairs. Why was I so terrified?

"Queer talk, yah?"

"Sorry?" I asked.

"That's what you're here for, right?"

I nodded. I found a chair and folded my whole bulky body into as small a shape as I could.

"How's everybody doing?"

Mutters and nods. A comment I couldn't make out. Some laughter.

"Most of you know me. I'm Shaz. I'm covering for Raquel. I'm not official or anything, none of us are, but I'm officially running this meeting today. Yes? Nothing too fancy. That's how we roll. I see some new people. Maybe we can go around and everyone can say hello, introduce themselves. Maybe let's do zodiac signs, too. And pronouns. And . . . what would be good?"

"Bumper cars."

"Laser tag."

"How about . . . if you had to be an animal, what

kind of animal would you be? Is that dumb? That's dumb but we're doing it."

We started to Shaz's left.

"Hey, everyone. I'm Taidgh, like tie-dye. I use they-them. I'm a lizard, I guess . . ."

Taidgh turned and gestured to the person beside them.

"Hey, everyone." I immediately recognized the blue hair. It was the person I'd seen at *Querelle*. "I'm Andre. He-him. I'm a grasshopper." He flipped an invisible ponytail off his shoulder. A few people laughed. "And a Gemini."

As we went around the circle, I started to get more and more worried. What was I doing here? What would I tell them? If I said my stupid secret name, did I think everything would suddenly become clear? Would they think I was joking? Would they think I was making fun of them? Why did I even bother? I was almost ready to leave—but then it was my turn.

"Hey, everyone," I said, in a voice that was probably too quiet. "I think I'm probably an eagle?" I cleared my throat and tried to talk louder. "I'm a Leo. Um. What else?"

"What's your name, dear?" Shaz prompted.

I swallowed.

"Sasha Masha."

A pause. "Can you say that again, dear? I don't think we caught it."

"Sasha Masha. My name's Sasha Masha."

Shaz's lips parted a little bit, as if she wanted to smile, but then someone else in the circle called out, "Yes, Sasha Masha, werk, Sasha Masha," and everyone burst out laughing.

But no one questioned it.

"And what pronouns do you use, Sasha Masha?"

I hadn't thought that far ahead. Seventeen years of reflex kicked in.

"Oh, um. He-him, I guess."

"Great. Thanks."

For most of the next hour I tried to listen, but my heart was racing. I was stuck on the name thing.

I asked myself: Did I feel any different?

I couldn't tell. It did feel good to say aloud.

Sasha Masha. My name is Sasha Masha.

I didn't feel like I had been reborn, but I felt different.

During a final announcements section, Andre asked if anyone could give him a ride home. I raised my hand. Andre nodded, gave a thumbs-up.

"Thanks, Sasha Masha," Shaz said, like it was no big deal.

Chapter 10

~~~~~~~~~~

I tripped on the sidewalk and Andre caught me by the arm.

"You all right?"

"Yeah."

My hand was shaking as I put the key in the ignition, and as soon as the car grumbled to life, so did the Spanish radio in a blast of drums and synth. I switched it off as quickly as I could. What was he going to think of this white boy blaring Spanish radio?

"Sorry," I said, but I wasn't sure for what.

"You're fine," Andre said, and smiled. He put his

address in my phone, and we drove for a while in silence.

"Were you obsessed with *Querelle* or what?"

It took me a second to register what he was saying.

"You were there, right? When they showed it? This was like, a while ago. I saw you there. You were there, right?" Andre said. He was turning his head to look at me, but I kept my eyes on the road.

"I was there," I replied, allowing a half smile at the corner of my mouth.

"Okay, thank God," Andre said, and flopped back in his seat. "I was worried I was losing my mind. I spent that whole meeting staring at you, thinking, *Where have I seen that face?* I'm sorry if I was creeping you out, Sasha Masha."

"No, not at all."

"But were you not obsessed? Did obsession not follow?"

I smiled a little more. "Obsession followed."

"I wouldn't have guessed that Fassbinder would be the most natural match for Genet." The names were coming a little too fast and I wasn't sure I knew what he was talking about. "'Cause a lot of Fassbinder is very . . . German." He looked to me. "I guess partly because Fassbinder is German. Genet is French. But not French like fancy. Have you seen other Fassbinder?"

I gathered that Fassbinder was the person who had made the movie. Maybe the director or the writer. Genet was someone else, also involved somehow.

"No."

"Have you read any Genet?"

"No."

"Okay, stop the train, I'm sorry, right now. Right now. No Genet? What kind of a queer are you? Pardon my French. You don't actually have to pull over the car. But you have to know Genet! Jean Genet? Saint Genet? *Our Lady of the Flowers*? *The Thief's Journal*?"

I shook my head. I couldn't help but get swept up in Andre's excitement.

"I'm bringing you my copy of *The Thief's Journal*. No—*Our Lady of the Flowers*. That's the place to start. God, what else? No, okay, I'm making you a reading list. I already have like . . . three . . . things on it. Five. I'll bring you my copy of *Our Lady of the Flowers*

90

and I'll write a reading list on the inside front cover. If your parents are weird about things like that, you can pretend you're reading *Harry Potter* or something. Though—and riddle me this, Dumbledore—why is no one talking about how queer *that* book is?"

"I don't know," I said. "*Harry Potter* is queer?"

"It's, well—no, it's not really that queer. I get carried away sometimes."

He took a deep breath. Andre was a senior at another high school, Patterson, though he was a year older than most of the kids in his class. He'd taken a semester off sophomore year, then another one junior year ("health stuff"). Most of his friends were in college now. I asked if he'd ever met Mabel at the Lavender Ladder, but he said he didn't think so. He hadn't been coming to meetings that long.

Soon we were outside his house. We swapped numbers, and I said I'd try to come to the next meeting.

"Tell me—one good thing about tonight. One thing you're holding on to."

"Oh," I said. "I guess I'm holding on to how nice it can be . . . to say who you are."

"Definitely," he replied. "Always a plus."

"And how about you?" I asked. "One good thing from the meeting."

"That's easy," he replied. "A new friend."

I turned and looked him in the eye. Sasha Masha might have wanted to kiss him. A wish big and bright as a sun rose inside of me, and it only got brighter, warmer, hotter as I looked at his face, his lips, his smile.

But I was Alex still, not Sasha Masha, and I was dating Tracy. I said good night.

Chapter 11

The next day in school, a Wednesday, Tracy was in a great mood. She swooped into English class and dropped a postcard on my desk.

"It's back," she said. "Have you ever been?"

The postcard was advertising the twenty-seventh annual Apple Cider Festival, somewhere out in Anne Arundel County. I hadn't been, no.

"It's super cheesy, but I kind of love it," Tracy said. "There's bobbing for apples and cider doughnuts and pig races. And lots of really stupid apple puns. It's this weekend. Want to come with me?"

"Of course," I told her, and smiled.

Except now that I was seeing her, my mind was racing with what had happened the night before. What *had* happened? Nothing. Nothing happened. I shouted something and ran out of the house. I went to a meeting. I tried out a name. I made a new friend. My parents were worried when I got home, but not too worried. Everything was the same. Nothing had to change. Did I want things to change? I couldn't tell. Or, no. I didn't. Not yet. How could I want things to change if I didn't know what changing meant?

"This coming week is basically my favorite week of the year. The apple festival and Halloween. What more could a person ask for?" she said, and the second bell rang, and she rumpled my hair and went back to her seat. Ms. Lewiston was lecturing on the background for our next book, but I couldn't focus long enough to pay attention. I was waiting to feel my phone buzz, hoping Andre would text me.

I felt weird and distracted at lunch. Jo, Jen, Tracy, and James were having an involved debate about whether people were essentially one way or another.

They were talking about serial killers at one point, and then at another point they were talking about whether men were always aggressive and women always wanted to come to consensus. My dad loved to point out that "science showed" how men had one evolutionary strategy and women had another; how men were conquerors and women were consensus builders. But I didn't particularly feel like volunteering that factoid on his behalf.

"Apparently seahorses are hermaphrodites," I said, since I felt like I should contribute.

"Interesting," James replied.

The next night I went over to Tracy's to do homework and have dinner. Tracy's mom usually made a big salad and this roast chicken that was a little sweet and a little spicy. We'd spend the time before the meal sprawled on Tracy's bed, or Tracy's couch, working and talking; talking about work, sometimes, but also just talking. Planning dates or speculating about the future. Tonight, though, something felt off. It was almost like I could tell we were going to have a fight.

She closed her laptop and sat up suddenly on the bed.

"Mister Alexi! We have to figure out what we're wearing for Halloween!" she said.

"Do we?" I asked. I lifted the corner of my mouth in what I thought would be a coy smile, but I knew there was an edge of sarcasm buried under there somewhere.

"We do, we do," Tracy said. "Are you a big costume person?"

"Not really," I replied.

Tracy looked off into space for a bit, and then apologized. "Sorry. I just think I'm hitting a work wall."

"That's all right," I said. There was a pregnant pause. I wondered if I should tell Tracy about my name. Maybe that would help. "I'm gonna keep going on this history outline, if that's okay."

"Sure," Tracy said, without much conviction. I stared into my history textbook and then at my laptop screen. I could feel her watching me.

Then she got up and started picking up clothes and folding them.

"Do you mind if I put on some music?" she asked.

"No, that's fine," I said, without looking up.

"I think food will be ready soon."

"Cool. I just want to try to get to the end of this section."

"Okay. I'm not trying to stop you." And she turned on the clock radio by her bed, the music low.

Neither of us said anything to each other, and pretty soon her mom called us downstairs. We filled our plates. Tracy's dad wanted to know how the debate team was faring. Antony kept saying, "Whatsup, cuz?" It was his response to everything, and eventually he got sent to his room. Tracy barely looked at me all dinner.

Afterward we went back upstairs, and Tracy closed the door behind us.

"Do you not like me anymore? Do you think I'm boring?"

"No," I said, a little startled. "Not at all. I just wanted to work. And," I added, my voice very soft, "I'm just not that into Halloween."

Tracy didn't say anything. She moved around her room, looking for things to do with her hands.

"Look, Alex," she said. "I get it. You miss Mabel.

Mabel's a lot, I don't know, cooler than me. Your life was probably a lot more interesting before you started dating me—"

"Tracy," I interrupted her. "That's not true at all—"

"What is it then, Alex?" She stood straight up and faced me. "If that's not why you've been so weird lately, then *what is it*?"

I started muttering, "It's nothing, I'm just, I have a lot of work to do . . . and I wasn't really in the mood to . . ."

I trailed off.

Sasha Masha. I couldn't tell her. Not yet.

"I don't think you're being honest with me," she said.

I was afraid of what I'd reveal if I opened my mouth, so I just shook my head and looked at my feet.

Tracy waited. Then she sat down on the couch. Her legs were crossed and her back was straight and her eyes were shooting daggers at me. "I don't think you understand," she said, "how shitty it feels being with you sometimes."

That was news. Maybe my distraction had been

more obvious than I realized. I tried not to let her see my eyes.

"There are days," she went on, "when you are so sweet, and caring, and I just feel so lucky. But then there are days . . ." She caught her breath and started to cry a little bit. I looked up at her. I'd never seen Tracy cry. "I'm sorry, I'm being stupid."

I shook my head no and came over and sat by her. I took her hand, but she took it back and laid it in her lap. I was afraid to say anything. And then she looked at me.

"I don't know if it's a good idea to keep doing this," she said. "What we're doing."

A moment of silence stretched into two moments. Three. I felt at a loss for words. I felt afraid. What could I say? Tracy stood up and blew her nose. She had stopped crying. She didn't look at me, but she went back to picking up clothes, folding them, putting away the books that had ended up sprawled across the floor and the yellow couch.

I watched her a moment and then I covered my face. I didn't want her to see that I wasn't sad, or angry, or worried about breaking up. I was terrified about giving myself this name. It suddenly occurred to me that this name could change my life. I didn't understand it yet, but I knew it had great power. It had warped things, and would only keep warping things the longer I held on to it and kept it inside.

"Can we maybe still go to the apple festival this weekend?" I asked, finally, in a voice that sounded like it was coming from a tiny box inside me. "And then see where we're at?"

The best I could do. Pathetic. Holding on to a thread. Not ready to let go.

"Sure," Tracy replied, but she didn't meet my eyes.

Then I said it was late and Tracy agreed, and I packed up my books and my laptop and she gave me a ride home. We didn't talk in the car. Maybe neither of us had the energy to think anymore. There was still homework to finish.

Chapter 12

"What should I do, Murphy?"

He didn't answer. He fidgeted and then pounced on my hand when I tapped it on the carpet. He wrapped himself around my arm and chewed lightly at my knuckles. It was almost one in the morning. I'd come downstairs to try to finish my history outline. I hadn't been able to sleep.

It really did seem like some monstrous force was suddenly rampaging through my life. I didn't understand it, but I knew the name: *Sasha Masha*. I knew that I'd felt it that afternoon at Mabel's house, in the velvet dress. But a wall of impossibility loomed high in my mind.

Eventually I gave up on the history outline and went upstairs to bed.

At school the next day, everything seemed normal. It was a Friday. Tracy and I sat next to each other in English, and she reached over and put all her weight on my shoulder when she stood up to use the bathroom. I was so relieved not to be in the middle of a muddy breakup that I was extra smiley and chatty with her. I guess we were both so afraid of fighting that we steered as clear of it as we could. Most Friday nights we did something together, but tonight we had no plans, and so far neither of us had brought it up.

On my way to second period, I sent a text:

"hey andre, it's sasha masha, from the other night. any chance u want to hang out sometime?"

He texted me back just as second period was ending:

"hey Sasha Masha! yah totally. what r u doing next week?"

The warmth of it made me glad. I was supposed to wait to reply, though, right? I didn't want to seem too excited.

Tracy found me after last period. Habit at least had her walking me from my locker to the back lot where I'd catch the bus.

"I'm going to stay home tonight, if that's all right."

"Sure," I said, and nodded.

"Do you still want to go to the apple festival?"

"Yeah! I mean, if that's okay?"

"Are you sure?" She searched my eyes. "Is that actually what you want or is that what you think you should say?"

"Yeah," I said. "It is. I do. I want to go with you. Do you want to go with me?"

"I do," she said softly. "Yeah."

I rode the bus home, staring out the window at the sidewalks strewn with leaves and trash, the chain-link fences that wrapped around concrete yards. The bus moved west and north, and the smaller trees struggling to come up from squares in the pavement were replaced with bigger trees whose branches dimmed whole streets. The colors of the leaves reminded me of the color of the old T-shirts my dad loved to wear, shirts he'd had since college. Reds and oranges named after diners and rental car companies and minor league baseball teams. The leaves filled the gutters. When I got off the bus, I realized that for a while there, I had stopped thinking about Tracy or Andre or myself. I had stopped thinking about Sasha Masha. I had just been looking out at the world.

A gift. However fleeting.

As soon as I made it inside, I texted Andre.

"I think mostly just hanging out with my girlfriend"

"& homework lol"

"but if u feel okay to skip the lavender ladder"

"what about Tuesday"

"?"

Chapter 13

~~~~~~~~~~~~~~~~~~~~~~~~~~~~~~~~~

Saturday around noon, my mom, my dad, my mom's friend Janice, and I pulled up in front of Tracy's house. Janice was a college friend my mom had reconnected with on Facebook; she was visiting from Denver and staying with us for a few days. She made me wonder what my mom had been like at twenty. The Lewises met the Shapelskys and chatted in the sunshine on the lawn. Janice stood in the grass in her high-heeled boots and waved her ring-heavy fingers. I couldn't tell you how, but overnight our date had turned into a whole group expedition.

"Don't come back too late," Jennifer warned Tracy. "I'm making dinner."

Tracy and I could barely look each other in the face. When Tracy's mom squeezed my hand and waved goodbye, I had a feeling in my gut that I was making a mess of everything. I took the middle seat in the back between Janice and Tracy, and everyone had to move butts to get seat belts buckled. We rode through the fall-colored city, but I felt in no mood to daydream.

At the apple festival there were indeed apples and apple cider doughnuts and so many different stands trying to sell apple pie that I found myself craving anything salty and dry. We walked up and down the rows in a loose flock. My mom was telling Janice about my life.

"Alex is in his junior year, and he likes his school a lot—you like it a lot, right, Alex?"

"Yeah, I like it."

"He has the best English teacher," she said, "and the best history teacher." Janice nodded, looking back at me. "Which took a little bit of doing—"

"I wasn't going to get involved," my dad interjected, "but his mom thought—"

"You have to ask for certain teachers. You just have to. And anyway, it's been hard with his friend Mabel gone, but you seem to be holding up okay, no?"

"I'm all right." I shrugged.

"And how would you characterize your mother's life, Alex?" Janice asked, turning to me with a playful smile. "How would you describe *her* year so far?"

"Devastatingly stable," I replied.

Janice laughed out loud. I was weirdly thrilled at that.

Eventually Tracy and I split off from the grown-ups. We drifted down the hill toward the pig races.

The crowd around the miniature racetrack consisted of lots of little kids with painted faces and dirty fingers and their parents holding apple fritters on a stick or Styrofoam cups of hot apple cider. They cheered as someone on a microphone announced the lineup for the next race. George "Porker" Washington was going up against Thomas "Tubby" Jefferson, Alexander

"Ham Hock" Hamilton, and Benjamin "Butterball" Franklin.

There was a bang and four baby pigs came galloping out onto the sawdust track, little pink bodies bumping along in a hurry. It was over in a minute. "Ham Hock" Hamilton won.

I had a sinking feeling that I was about to spill everything to Tracy and that it wouldn't go well. I wasn't sure what I was spilling, really, but it seemed clear that I couldn't hold it in any longer. I had to tell her about Sasha Masha. I didn't know what I was going to say, and I didn't know what she would take it to mean. I was afraid. I was worried. The crowd was restless, and the next round of pigs were getting corralled into their starting cages. The man with the microphone was naming them, but I had trouble paying attention. And then it was as if a hand reached into my chest and turned my heart. I wasn't afraid anymore.

"Hey, will you come with me this way?" I held out my arm and waited for Tracy to take it. She didn't, but she indicated that she'd follow. I headed toward what seemed like the far edge of the festival grounds.

Bang! The gates were open for the second race, and the crowd was hollering.

Up ahead was a fence. I walked and could hear Tracy behind me. Uneven ground. Muddy earth covered in straw. Soon there would be nowhere else to go.

By the fence, we faced each other in the crisp, chilly air.

"What's going on, Alex?" Her voice was steely and level.

"I think that, um," I started to say. I felt like I was watching myself from outside my body. The muscles in my mouth were moving without my moving them. Time slowed down. The air smelled like apple pie and pig shit and I was standing there about to say something that I wasn't sure had any meaning. Something that would probably come off as pretty stupid. And I was about to say it with a straight face and my heart in my gut.

"I think my name's actually Sasha Masha."

"Okay," Tracy said, her face unchanged. "So what are you telling me?"

"Just that. That that's my name. It was starting to drive me a little crazy. And I thought I should tell you."

Tracy looked at me, searched my face for something else. For what I might say next. But I didn't say anything else. I just shrugged.

"You know what?" Tracy said. "I think I'm done with this. I don't know what this game is about, but I'm tired of feeling like you're playing with me. I'm gonna head home."

My mouth opened. "What do you mean?"

"I mean that I want to break up."

"Oh."

She looked at me an extra moment, and then she took out her phone and started texting someone. She seemed completely unemotional. But then I noticed that her hands were shaking. This wasn't the reaction I'd expected at all. I was too surprised to argue.

"Um," I said. "Who are you texting?"

"I'm texting Jo, to see if she can come pick me up."

And that's when I wished I could take it all back. I felt a huge sadness come flooding in, and all I could think about was wanting to make things better. *Never mind,* I wanted to tell her. *I didn't mean it. I don't know what I was thinking.* I wanted to wrap my arms around her, tell her it wasn't true. I wanted to drop it, simplify, get rid of the thing that didn't make sense. All of a sudden it didn't make sense to me either. *Don't worry,* I wanted to say. *I'm just me. I'm just Alex.* I wanted everything to feel as simple as it had that magic, endless afternoon by Lake Roland.

"No, Tracy, slow down. Let me explain."

"It sounded like you explained all you could explain. And frankly, I'm tired of asking for explanations and getting ones that don't make any fucking sense."

"Let's just go for a walk. And then we can all drive home together. My parents can drop you off."

"Are you insane? That sounds like the worst thing in the world." Tracy looked up at me. "The last thing I want to do is walk around this stupid pig-smelling place pretending we've been in a real relationship for the last two months instead of some fantasy I tricked myself into believing. Sometimes I think you're completely out of your mind."

I felt myself shrink. "Um," I said again. "I'm sorry."

"I think I'd like to have a moment to myself," she said. "And then I'm just going to go. Jo is going to come get me."

"What are you going to tell her?"

"I'm going to tell her that it's over. I'm going to tell her that I'm relieved."

"But what about . . . ?"

"About your name? Masha Pasha or whatever?" She glared at me. "I don't have much interest in dignifying that with a response."

"Can we just talk a little bit?"

"What is there to talk about? You said what you had to say." Tracy's hands were shoved resolutely in her pockets. Her feet were planted next to each other in the mud. Then she flinched and looked off toward where the pig races were continuing in endless rounds. "I'm sorry, I need to go."

"I didn't mean to hurt you," I said, but I said it too quietly and she was already walking away.

Chapter 14

The next day, Sunday, I slept till noon.

"Good morning, sleepyhead," my dad said when I came downstairs. "You must have been beat from all those apples and pig races."

"Yeah, I guess so."

When I'd found them after the races, I'd told them Tracy wasn't feeling well and had left the festival early.

"Have you heard from her? Is she feeling any better?" my dad asked.

"I think so," I said.

"That's good."

I poured myself a bowl of cereal and joined them around the table like nothing was wrong. My whole body felt like Mabel's and my favorite parking garage, the way it got empty and still at night. It was a kind of exhaustion, but it was a kind of relief, too.

Janice turned to me. "We're talking about our friend Terry," she clarified. "He just left his wife and sold his house and moved into a trailer in Wyoming."

"Ah," I replied.

"When people get to be our age, they sometimes flip out a little bit," my dad said to me by way of explanation. "Too many regrets."

My phone buzzed. It was a new text from Andre. Under the table I read:

"Tuesday yah"

"how about paper moon?"

I replied with a thumbs-up.

Eventually my mom pushed back from the table and proposed that they get on the road. "You sure you don't want to come, sweetie?" They were taking Janice to the Baltimore Museum of Art.

I shook my head.

After they were gone, I tried to focus on school-work. But my mind kept flooding with my own regrets. I wished I'd said more to Tracy. I wished I'd tried to explain. Still, I knew the damage had already been done. And anyway Tracy had once said it felt "shitty" being with me. I had been a bad, distracted boyfriend well before I brought up Sasha Masha.

Mabel called that afternoon. I told her that Tracy and I were over.

"Did you break up with her, or did she break up with you?"

"She broke up with me."

"But what happened? Did something happen?"

I took a deep breath and did my best to describe the situation.

"Well, first off, I think I want my name to be Sasha Masha."

"And that's why Tracy broke up with you?"

"Yes and no."

Even with Mabel I couldn't explain it very well.

"It's not about the name. But the name is also everything," I said.

"You sound like an insane religious leader," Mabel told me. "In a terrible movie."

"I know! It's awful."

"I mean, how would you describe it, this Sasha Masha–ness? This thing you're after. *I* get it. But I was there. And I'm me."

I tried, but my mind refused any other language. "I'm not . . . sure." I had a sudden wave of despair. "Ugh. I'm sorry."

"It's okay, my dear," Mabel said. "All in good time!"

Monday was Halloween and relentless chaos. It might have seemed like Halloween was a great day to try being someone new, but somehow I couldn't muster the right spirit. You couldn't walk down the hallway without bumping into someone's wings, or horns, or stuffed appendage. Maybe Sasha Masha wasn't the key to who I was after all. Maybe it was just my own stupid stuffed appendage.

Tracy wasn't there in English. Jo was wearing fairy wings. I thought about asking her if Tracy was okay, but then decided against it. In history I avoided eye contact with Jen, though probably that was because of her vampire cape and the trickle of blood at the corner of her mouth.

"Alex! What happened?" Mr. Wolper-Diaz asked me in the hallway. "You forget your costume?"

"Who knows?" I shrugged, and made myself smile.

Chapter 15

At lunch, I couldn't quite bring myself to sit alone. When I saw Jake Florieau on the other side of the room, I headed toward him.

"Hey, Jake."

"What's up, Shapelsky?"

"Okay if I join you?"

"Surely."

If he was surprised, he didn't show it. I had felt pretty lousy all day, so the way he slid his tray over to make room felt almost tender. It struck me that there could be something gentlemanly about Jake Florieau.

"What's new, Shapelsky?" he asked. "Seen any good movies lately?"

I sighed a chuckle of a sigh because all the movies I'd seen lately I'd seen with Tracy. "Eh," I replied. "Nothing that changed my life. You?"

"Nada," he said. Then he shrugged. "Hollywood must be dead."

From there we started talking about our favorite music documentaries. Then we were laughing about some of the concerts we'd gone to when we were freshmen. Jake remembered sitting with me outside some venue under the expressway scrubbing the back of his hand to get rid of the *X* that meant he was under twenty-one.

"And you were pretending the whole thing didn't make you nervous."

I smiled. "You're not wrong."

"Who *were* we?" he asked.

"What do you mean?"

"Like, who were those people? Are those people us?"

"I guess so," I replied, and took a mouthful of sandwich. I mumbled through bread and tuna. "I don't know what we were thinking."

"Well, maybe I didn't know what I was doing then, but I've got it all figured out now," Jake said with a sigh.

"Oh, sure."

We laughed. I wondered, a little ashamed, if I might have gotten in the habit of treating him coldly since we'd stopped hanging out freshman year. If I had, I'd made a mistake. I was especially grateful that all of lunch went by and he didn't once ask why I wasn't sitting with Tracy.

That night my parents put me on candy duty. I sat by the door with a big bowl of mini chocolate bars. The doorbell wouldn't stop ringing. Half the people were dressed as characters from some movie, in costumes they'd bought at a store. Didn't people make their own costumes anymore? Probably five people looked at my hoodie and jeans and judged my lack of Halloween spirit. "Who are you supposed to be? Yourself?" they'd say, as if that were some kind of original joke.

The next day after school I raced through math homework and scarfed down dinner so I could meet Andre. I knew I'd have to tell my parents eventually that Tracy and I had broken up, but I wanted to get one more night out of the lie. So I asked to borrow the car and said I was going to Tracy's.

"Say hi for me," my dad called as I headed out the door.

It was after nine, but the Papermoon was crowded. I didn't see Andre, so I got a booth. The walls were painted bright colors, and there were mannequin limbs hanging from the ceiling like chandeliers. The whole place smelled like french fries and maple syrup. Andre slid into the booth across from me, a few minutes late, and flopped his head on the table.

"Sasha Masha," he said, face in his arms. "What a day."

I laughed. He sat up and smiled back at me.

"Everything okay?" I asked.

"Well," he began, "I don't know how things were at your school, but at my school it was a *messy* Halloween. This big group of sophomores had a plan to dress up as a school of dolphins, and they were going to swarm the stage during the assembly. But the thing is the soccer team *also* had a plan to be sea creatures, except like vampire sea creatures, so they had all this fake blood. Then they got in a fight with the sophomores. At first it was a joke but you have to picture like twenty-five people in big bulky dolphin and whale and octopus suits trying to get off a stage and all slipping and sliding in fake blood. This one kid got a concussion."

"Oh no!" I said, trying not to laugh.

"Yeah . . . he's okay," Andre concluded. "And otherwise none of the teachers made us do anything, so that was cute. Did you dress up?"

"Not really."

"Why not?"

"I . . . didn't really feel like it," I said lamely.

He smiled anyway, shrugged, and looked around. "Have you been here before?"

I hadn't. Andre said that everything was excellent. We both ordered decaf coffee and dessert. Bread pudding for me and apple pie for Andre.

"So, but I don't know anything about you, Sasha Masha," Andre said, once the waiter had cleared the menus. "What's your deal?"

"I don't know. I'm a junior. I like movies."

"And do you come to the Lavender Ladder all the time, or . . . ?"

"Not all the time. But I like it there. My friend Mabel used to go a lot."

"You mentioned this person. But they don't go anymore?"

"She moved. To Pittsburgh."

"I see. And you have a girlfriend?"

"We, um, broke up. Actually."

"Sasha Masha! I'm sorry to hear. How are you doing?"

"I'm doing all right," I said.

"When did this happen? Like, yesterday? I feel like you were just telling me about plans to hang out with her."

"Yeah."

The waiter brought us coffee, steaming in heavy porcelain mugs with a spoon in each one. Between us he placed a small pitcher of milk with condensation beading on the metal surface.

"Can I ask," Andre began, licking the spoon as he pulled it out of his coffee, "the story of your name?"

"Sure," I said, trying to think where to start.

"Is it a family name?"

"Oh! No," I said, laughing. "It's, um, just something I picked for myself."

"And what made you pick it? Does it have a special meaning?"

"No, I just . . ." And I took a deep breath. "It came to me one day when I was hanging out with Mabel. We were trying on these clothes her aunt gave her, and I put on this dress and it just . . . it was like something huge clicked into place. And it came to me. And I've been thinking about it a lot lately, that name. For a while I thought it was because I missed Mabel, but I think it's actually trying to tell me something about myself."

"The name is?"

"The name, yeah."

He nodded. "And what is it trying to tell you?"

"I don't know, really!" I threw my hands up. "That's the part I feel confused about."

"Well, you've just got to listen to her, babe. She'll tell you what she wants to tell you."

"I guess," I said.

"Do you want to know my full name?"

"Sure."

"Andrew Charles Nickleson Norteño III. Which, yeah, is great. Very, like, imperial. But as a kid I was Andrew. Always Andrew."

"I see."

"Yeah. Two years ago I was a different person than I am now."

"What happened?"

"I don't know. The whole package needed a little *zhush*. You seem like the strong and steady type, so maybe you won't relate to this. But I feel like every two years is good for a little *zhush*."

"Sure."

"And I feel like teenagers get a bad rap for changing things up all the time. We're fake, or we're insincere, or we're superficial. But if you do it to please yourself, what's insincere about that?"

I must have looked a little concerned, because Andre asked me why I was scrunching my eyebrows.

"No, I just . . . ," I started to say, and wrapped my hands around my warm mug. "I know what you mean. And I feel a little dumb, because even just thinking about this name, it's been so intense, weirdly. Why does it feel so important? And why does it feel so hard?"

"But of course it's hard, Sasha Masha. There's this thing that matters to you. For whatever reason, it does. Doesn't it?"

I nodded acknowledgment, with a little bit of a shrug.

"So? That's what it is," he said.

"But what does it *mean*?" I wanted to know.

126

"I don't know, Sasha Masha. That's a question for you."

"I just feel weird thinking about it so much, because it probably makes zero sense to most other people I know."

"Sure," he said. "People are gonna laugh. They're not gonna get it. They're gonna tell you you're making a fuss. Or trying to shove something in their faces. But you're not trying to be heavy about it, you're just trying to be you."

"I know! But why do I feel so heavy about it all the time? I don't know what I'm doing . . ."

"You know what you're doing," Andre said, and leaned across the table. He put his finger down in front of me. "You know exactly what you're doing. There's just too much noise from all around here." He indicated the restaurant and beyond it the world.

Our food came. With whipped cream.

"Speaking of noise . . . ," Andre muttered.

"I don't know," I said. "Right now it seems important to focus on the dessert situation."

For a while we did just that.

I felt self-conscious that we'd been talking so much about me. So when we'd both had a chance to dig in, I changed the subject.

"Um, can I ask when you first came out? Not to assume that you're queer, or, I just . . ."

"I don't know if I was ever in," he said, and laughed. "I used to cut out pictures of boys in swimsuits and tape them to my wall. This was like fourth grade. It was probably clear, if you know what I mean."

"I wish I'd been like that!"

"What, gay?"

"Well, that too," I said, and blushed a little.

Andre laughed.

"I think what I mean," I said, "is that I feel like I was on autopilot for most of my life. That I just took for granted the person the world told me I was. And I feel like it might have been easier to shake that up a little when I was a kid."

"How old are you now, ninety-two?"

"No, I know, I just . . ."

"I don't know about easy or not easy. It's just different."

"Or, not easy, but . . ."

"You're just doing this now, Sasha Masha. Now's your time. And you're doing it. So what else do you have to worry about?"

"I guess," I said, and sighed.

"Don't sigh at me. You're too pretty to sigh."

I blushed and muttered something like *you're very kind.*

"Can I try some of your bread pudding?" he asked, pointing with a fork.

"Of course. But only if I can try some of your apple pie."

Eventually we paid and headed to my dad's car. Andre had taken the bus here, so I told him I'd give him a ride home. This time I felt less stressed about what was Alex and what was Sasha Masha. As we drove, we rolled the windows down and let the cold air blow against our faces.

"So, but do you have any sense," he asked me, once we were on the road, "who it is you want to be, beyond the name? Or that's a bad way of asking it. What else do you know about Sasha Masha?"

"It's all a little fuzzy," I said. "And I think I want to figure it out a bit more before I tell too many people. I don't have the clearest idea for myself yet."

"Sure," Andre said.

"So we'll see."

We drove for a while in silence. I could tell he was considering something.

"One little bit of advice," he said, after a moment. "If I may."

"Sure, of course."

"You seem like you're a real brain person. You keep it all in here." He gestured to his head. "Don't think about this one too much, okay? Just . . . let it happen."

When we got to his place, the street was dark, and there was a dog barking somewhere. A light glowed from under the front blinds, then flickered and changed colors. Someone was probably still up, watching TV.

"Thanks for the ride," he said.

"Of course," I said. "Thanks for meeting me."

"Are you kidding? Now that you're missing a Mabel, I want you to meet everybody. What are you doing Thursday?"

"Oh—um. Nothing. Why?"

"I'll see if my friends Coco and Green are around. They're amazing. They're my fairy godmothers. Want to meet them?"

"Yeah, of course."

"Great. Thursday then. And also—wait—fuck." And his eyes lit up. "Miss Thing. Is Saturday."

"What's Miss Thing?"

"Miss Thing is . . ." He tapped the dashboard. "Just don't make any plans Saturday night. We're going to Miss Thing. Will you come?"

"Sure," I said, my face hot and my smile probably too big.

"Not that you have any choice," Andre said, smiling back. "All right. I'm leaving."

I watched him make his way up the walk. My whole body was tingling.

I pulled out my phone for the first time since I'd

arrived at the Papermoon and saw that I had a voice mail and two texts from my dad: "Pls call me," one said. The other was, "Will you please confirm that you are still alive?"

"Yeah," I texted back.

"Sorry"

"On my way now—had to drop somebody off."

"Drive safe," he replied. "See you soon."

"Sorry," I said again, as I came in the door. It was 12:32. He was sitting up reading. The house was quiet. He put down his book.

"All good?" he asked. Which was what he said when he was mad at you but didn't want to say it yet.

"Yeah, I just . . ." And I trailed off.

"You just what?"

"No, I'm sorry it's so late." I realized that I might have just painted myself into a corner. I had told him I was going over to Tracy's. And then I'd said I was dropping someone off. Who was I dropping off twenty-five minutes away?

My dad sighed and pushed himself forward in his chair. He rubbed his eyes under his glasses.

"There is the issue of your provisional license, and the issue of a ticket if you'd gotten caught driving after midnight. But mostly I was just a little rattled to find out you weren't telling the truth about where you were going tonight, Alex."

"Oh," I said lamely. "Why? Did you . . ."

"I ran into Tracy's dad at the grocery store, and we were just chatting, you know, being proud of our kids, and all that."

"Oh," I said, even more lamely. My heart was in my ankles. "Yeah."

"And it's okay if you don't want to talk about your relationship with us, you know? That's your business. But I'll just say that the thoughts that went through my head when I didn't know where you were—I was doing my best not to sensationalize, but when you have kids, you'll understand that it's not a great feeling."

"I . . . yeah. I'm sorry."

"Another half hour and I would have gone into panic mode."

"I know, I'm sorry."

"Will you tell me, in brief at least, what the hell is going on?"

"I just . . . ," I began. "I met this friend. And we went to a diner and had pie and coffee and we were just talking. I lost track of the time."

He stared at me a long moment.

"All right," he said, and looked at his lap a second like he was thinking. Then he inhaled and heaved himself out of his chair.

"I'm going to go to bed now, and you probably should, too, but I hope you'll tell me a bit more about what's going on at some point," he said. "I'm glad you're okay. I'm glad you seem relatively sober . . ."

"No, Dad, I'm totally . . ."

"Great. No. I believe you." He stood and came toward me. He put his hand on my shoulder. "I feel like I know you pretty well, Alex. And it just threw me, I have to say." He turned to go upstairs. "I started to wonder if I had you all wrong."

Chapter 16

"You have a glow to you, Shapelsky," Jake said as I sat down. "A good night last night? Or you just get your English paper back?"

"You think you're very funny, don't you?"

"I know I am."

Lunch with Jake was becoming the only part of the school day I actually enjoyed.

"Have you ever been to this place, the Lavender Ladder?" I asked him.

"No, what's that?"

I explained meeting Andre there, and told him that

he was who I'd been hanging out with the night before.

"Would you believe it," Jake began, "if I told you that I literally don't know any queer people?"

"Wait, really?"

"There's Tyler Lort and Jae Holron the year below us, but I'd say they are only marginally out."

"Yeah, I didn't know about them . . ."

"And I get the feeling most people think I'm this homosexual demon boy with vast sexual experience. But actually I'm like Drew Barrymore."

"What do you mean?"

"Never been kissed."

"Jake!"

"Don't act so horrified."

"No, I'm not horrified, I'm just surprised."

"Is that a compliment or an insult? I'm not sure."

"No, you just always seemed so confident. I figured . . ."

Jake shrugged.

"So take me out," he said. "Is all I'm asking. Take me to meet your queers."

"I will," I said, looking at him, and realizing how much I'd assumed.

We ate for a while in silence.

"Hey, Jake?" I asked. "Do you have any advice about talking to your parents?"

"Like about what?"

"About personal stuff, I guess. Stuff you're nervous to talk about."

"I don't tell my parents anything. What do they need to know about my life?"

"I don't know, if it's a big thing. Like, what was it like coming out to your parents?"

"My parents think I'm straight, Shapelsky."

"Wait, really?"

"A shocker, I know. You'd think they were legally blind."

"No, I don't know."

"No, it's completely ridiculous. But they need to believe I'm straight, I guess. For their own twisted reasons. And I like having the space they give me, knowing I'm their good, Christian, heterosexual son."

"They really think that?"

"They think I have a girlfriend named Marta."

"Wow."

"What do you need to tell your parents?" he asked.

"It's this weird, kind of unusual thing . . ."

"You can be whatever you want to be, Shapelsky. I certainly won't judge."

I blushed. "No, I mean . . . maybe I don't need to tell them."

"There's no harm in trying," he said. "Just drop a hint or two. What's the worst that could happen?"

"I guess nothing too terrible."

"I've met your parents, Shapelsky. Your parents are not going to kick you out of the house. They might get very stressed out, but they're not going to disown you."

I sighed. "You're probably right."

I spent most of the rest of the day not paying attention in class, figuring out how I wanted to broach the subject. I couldn't just come right out with it, the way

I had with Tracy. I needed to introduce the concept slowly, and also get a sense of where I stood. I started to feel good about my plan on the bus ride home. I took my moment toward the end of dinner. My dad was scooping the last of the pasta onto his plate, and my mom was scraping the last of the salad toward the center of the bowl.

"Do you ever think," I began, "about how most teenagers have this big moment where they reinvent themselves? Like they become goth, or they get really into exercise?"

My mom carried the bowl into the kitchen.

My dad studied my face. "We're not letting you get a tattoo," he responded.

"No, no, that's not . . . I just wonder about it sometimes," I muttered.

"Are you thinking of taking up a new hobby?" my mom asked from the kitchen. "I hear that very hip kids are getting into knitting."

"No," I said. "I wonder about changing my name."

My dad chuckled.

My mom came back in, wiping her hands on a dish towel. "Is that really something you think about?" she asked, concerned.

"Sometimes, I don't know."

"What would you change your name to? Al or something? Xander?" my dad volunteered.

I flinched. A moment of doubt. And then I said it. "Like, maybe . . . Sasha Masha."

They both looked at me, mouths open, completely surprised a moment. At least I'd gotten their attention. Then they both started to laugh.

"Oh, sweetie," my mom said. "I thought you were serious for a second."

"Yeah, I don't know," I said, trying to cover up how flustered I felt. My dad shook his head and chuckled. "I don't know where I got that one."

And I felt very far away from both of them.

Mabel was excited I'd been hanging out with someone from the Lavender Ladder.

"Blue hair! He sounds cute. Is he cute?"

"Yeah," I said. "He's cute."

"Nice work, Alexidore. When do you see him next?"

"Tomorrow."

"Tomorrow!"

"Yeah. Tomorrow."

"That's so soon."

"It is. I'm a little obsessed. But I don't wanna talk about me. Let's talk about you."

"What about me?"

"I don't know, tell me about school. Tell me about your people."

And she told me about the five other people she hung out with most days after school. Last week they made tamales together. Next week they were going to a concert. One of them was Alice. Mabel was crushing hard.

"I like it here, Alexidore. I have to say."

"I'm glad," I told her. "I miss you a lot, but I'm glad."

"Me too. I miss you, too," she said. "How about Sasha Masha? How's she? Is that all right, to call her 'she'?"

"I don't know," I said. "But yeah, I guess it's all right."

"What's going on?"

"I almost talked to my parents about it tonight, but then I got a weird vibe and chickened out."

"That's okay. Truly. Parents are hard." She took a big inhale and sighed.

I was tired of talking about it. I just wanted to be living it. And I wished I knew what living it meant.

"I think I'm gonna go to bed," I told her.

"All right. Sleep well, Sasha Masha."

"Thanks, Maybelline. Love you."

Chapter 17

~~~~~~~~~~~~~~~~

"Is it okay if I use the car tonight?"

"Why, do you have plans?"

"I might go hang out with this new friend," I said as casually as I could.

They exchanged a look I couldn't read, but then they said it was fine and just to make sure my phone was charged so they could get in touch with me. They asked me my friend's name.

"Andrew," I told them.

My mom wanted me to write down Andrew's

parents' names and their number, but I said I'd never met them and it would be weird to ask. Eventually she nodded and said okay. "Just—take care of yourself, sweetie, okay? Don't do anything unsafe."

I told them okay thanks and I'd see them in a few hours.

Andre's neighborhood looked completely different in the last light of day. There were kids' tricycles on the lawns and signs in the grass, reminding dog walkers to curb their dogs.

Andre came out to meet me and said Coco and Green didn't live far.

"Coco used to host this performance night at the Lavender Ladder—that's how we met. I guess Coco's my drag mother. But then we started hanging out outside of that. Green's amazing, too."

"You do drag?"

"Eh, sometimes. Not so much anymore. But sometimes."

"That's cool."

"Anyway, mostly I wanted you to meet them because I think it's hard to do what you're doing without a little bit of, um . . . *context*." He looked at me. "Does that make sense?"

"I think so."

"It's just up here on the left."

We pulled up in front of a stretch of duplex houses—one porch, two front doors. Even in the dusky light you could tell that one half of the building was painted a staid gray and the other was bright green with orange trim. A man in jeans and a tiny black T-shirt under an open silk robe opened the door.

"My dears! Come in!"

I smiled and ducked past. I could feel him scanning my face. A round, furry belly poked out from under his shirt. He seemed like he might be in his late fifties—older than my parents. Andre said, "Hi, Coco," and gave him a hug.

"Ah, *mademoiselle*! Please!" He was calling after me. *Mademoiselle*. I didn't object.

"Shoes off, please, *por favor*," Coco clarified, with a winning smile. "I don't think we know each other."

"No, I'm Al—," I started to say, but I was bent over untying my shoes, so Andre chimed in.

"This is my new friend, Sasha Masha."

"A pleasure, Sasha Masha. I'm Coco."

He said my name rather solemnly and put his hands on my shoulders and kissed me on each cheek.

"These are the most astonishing biscuits!"

A voice from another room. A timer was going off.

"They look good?"

"They look astonishing!"

"Well, just put them on a plate, honey!" Andre led me into the kitchen and introduced me to Green as Green pulled said biscuits out of the oven, turned off the timer, and arranged things on the counter. Green was a little taller than Coco, but not by much—a green striped shirt, baggy, and a wispy little mustache. He seemed about the same age.

"Go go go go go sit in the living room," he urged.

We settled in on a couch and plush chairs, piled high with pillows, and Green brought in a whole succession of foods: biscuits, jam, tortilla chips, salsa, baby carrots, oatmeal raisin cookies from a Tupperware. I leaned into a pillow on a sheet on the couch.

"I love these baby carrots, Green," Coco said as Green settled in to join us.

"Yes, baby carrots are in season this time of year."

"She has a magnificent deadpan," Coco said, turning to me.

"Oh, do I? What else do I have?"

"Well, let me see. You have a nice neck."

Green *mm*ed appreciatively and then leaped up to bring in one last thing—a bowl of grapes. Andre passed me food and Green offered beers, but Coco objected and retracted the offer, proposing ginger ale or Coke instead ("These are children, my dear!"). I said I'd have some ginger ale and Andre said he'd have some, too. Green went to get them and Coco turned his attention to me. He was crunching a carrot.

"Is this a new friend? Sasha Masha, you said?"

"Yeah, Sasha Masha's awesome," Andre said.

"And do you ever speak for yourself, Sasha Masha?"

"Yeah," I said. "I do, sometimes."

"Well, that's good. How do you know Andre?"

"We met at . . . a group. This group thing. At the Lavender Ladder?" I kept turning to look at Andre, as if he needed to approve. Coco's direct gaze made me squirm a little. I felt like I wasn't the person I wanted to be with him.

"What kind of a group?"

"It's like a teen group? Would you say? For queer teens?"

"And it's a knitting circle, or . . . ?"

"Be nice, Coco," Green called from the kitchen.

"Who, me? Oh, I'm just giving Sasha Masha a hard time. I know the group."

Andre swooped in. "I just wanted Sasha Masha to meet you because he's at the beginning of a journey. Finding his way. Is that fair to say?" I nodded.

"I see," Coco said. "I do think Sasha Masha will have to learn to speak for Sasha Masha's self at *some* point, however."

"Leave the child alone!" Green called again from the kitchen.

Coco leaned in to me. "I'm not nearly as terrible as they all make me out to be. You realize that, my dear?"

I nodded.

"So what's this journey you're on?"

"I guess I figured out this name, Sasha Masha, not too long ago. But now I have to figure out the rest of it."

"A name, a name," Coco said thoughtfully. "So is this a drag name?"

"I don't think so. I think it's just me."

"I see. And who are you?"

"That's the thing. I'm trying to figure that out."

Green popped in from the kitchen. "Did you ever think about trying a Russian accent?"

My face got hot.

"No," I said. "But I'm not sure if that's quite what I'm after."

"Sure, all right," Green said, waving his hands and lifting his eyebrows and wandering back to the kitchen. "No harm in trying, though. I always say . . . try it all . . ."

Andre intervened. "Mostly I wanted Sasha Masha to know that he comes from a tradition," he said. "That he doesn't have to do this in a void."

"Well," Coco replied, "you know me, always happy to fill a void."

He looked back and forth between our faces.

"Look at the two of you! So deadly serious! Green, when was the last time you saw such serious young faggots? If there's one lesson I have to impart it's that you need to lighten up a little bit."

"Who, us?" Andre asked, out of the side of his mouth.

"Yes, you. Serious as chickens." Coco sighed. "And this is a serious piece of advice, so listen up: a sense of the absurd is *essential*. If you want to be ready for a *fight*—"

"Dear Coco," Green called from the kitchen again. "She's always spoiling for a fight."

"But it *is* a fight, you know? And not for chump change either. This is where you little chicks need to wake up to what's going on in the world. We're the ones who can see *beyond*. And they don't want us to

see beyond. They pat us on the head and tell us we can get married, and put on uniforms, and go shoot brown people overseas. But is that really the best we can imagine for our lives? We have a chance to build something totally different, we who feel differently, who live differently, who see that the way things are isn't the way they have to be. We have a chance to build toward a place where kids aren't locked away in prisons forever and where people have enough food to eat. Is the limit of our imaginations gonna be a goddamn wedding cake? Because don't get it twisted, they don't give a fuck about us, the Johns in suits, they'll brand their shit with the rainbow flag come pride month and they'll pay lip service to 'equality' or the HRC or whatever cis-rich bullshit, but when it comes to actually questioning the foundations of the world, they cling to the status quo and their nuclear families like some kind of terrified animal . . . Do you think they're gonna worry about our sorry faggot asses when they feel the things they've hoarded for years slipping away from them?"

"I think it's getting better, though," Andre said. "Don't

you think? There's a ways to go, but it's getting better. With representation of queer people in the media . . ."

Green came in with two tall glasses of ginger ale, and I thanked him under my breath.

"Representation is chump change, darling! I'm sorry to break it to you, dear. People who hold power don't like to put themselves at risk. And that's why queer people have generally been the visionaries. Because when your everyday *life* is a risk, you start to think about it all differently. You start to realize that organizing your days around keeping yourself protected is dumb as shit, and that there's a whole universe of meaning and connection when you get beyond that."

"I agree with you," Andre replied. "But I just think there are young people out there who don't know queer people exist, who don't know about this as a possibility. *And* you have queer people getting work being themselves in industries where they didn't use to be able to—"

Coco waved his hand. "Yes. Please. By all means. I'll never object to a girl getting paid. But I've had my heart broken too many times to think that visi-

bility means everything. I don't think it changes who steps up and who stands back. Where were the white cis faggots at Stonewall? And where are they now, with Black and Brown trans sisters getting murdered in the dozens? For some people, visibility is about saving a life. And for other people, it's about making things more comfortable. But again, my dears, it's not about comfort. Safety, yes, please. But comfort? Comfort is overrated. As far as I'm concerned, life is about being alive and being connected to our fellow creatures. Full stop. And your generation is making it worse with your serious faces and goddamn safe spaces and trigger warnings . . . Hello, my darlings! Loosen up! Live a little! Suck a dick! Tell a joke! Fall in love! Show up to start trouble when it's necessary and don't whine when the world doesn't hold your hand!"

Andre was shaking his head, but he was smiling. It seemed clear that they'd had a version of this argument many times before. Green grinned. "Tell us what you really feel, will you?"

Coco sighed and tossed an imaginary mane of hair. "I know. I get . . . swept away."

Then turned to me. "Do you know Marsha P. Johnson?"

I shook my head.

"Sylvia Rivera?"

I shook my head again.

"A crime." He turned to Andre. "You realize you have some work to do, correct?"

Andre laughed. "I do."

As conversation turned to other things, I looked around the room. It was covered with posters, and paintings, and books, and paper ornaments, and silk flowers, and a few drawings of naked men. Green had put on some music by then. He and Coco sipped their beers, and Andre and I slurped our ginger ale, and before long we had finished the carrots and the tortilla chips and the oatmeal raisin cookies. Green asked Andre how school was going, and Andre talked about how he and his friend Michelle were getting into writing songs. I could feel my face glowing. Here I was, wrapped in the heart of one of the warmest, coziest homes I'd ever visited, and I never wanted to leave.

"Sasha Masha," Andre said, "let me show you the hall of ancestors."

It was just a regular hallway, really. Off the living room. A long wall covered in framed photos. Some looked recent, others looked ten years old, twenty, fifty—a hundred.

"Coco's going to quiz us all," Green said as he and Coco joined us in front of the images.

"I don't have to quiz anybody," Coco insisted. "And anyway, I don't want to put Sasha Masha on the spot. We can just pay homage."

"*Andre* knows who some of these people are, of course," Green said.

"Some . . . that's James Baldwin," Andre said. "And that's Oscar Wilde."

"Yes!"

"And that's . . . David Wojnarowicz."

"Yes . . ."

"Who's David Wojna . . . ?" I asked.

"You'll have to go home and look him up, my dear," said Coco.

Andre explained in a low voice. "He was an artist," he said.

"Is that it, baby doll? That's all you've got?" Coco was scanning the wall with intensity and pride.

"No, I've got a few more. Okay." Andre was scanning the wall, too. It was a dim hallway, and crowded, but all the faces started to vibrate, somehow, as we looked at them and said their names.

"Walt Whitman," Andre said.

"Yes," Coco said.

"Joan of Arc?"

"Yep."

"I think that's Lorraine Hansberry?"

"Yes!"

"And Harvey Milk . . . But then I start to get . . . These other people look familiar, but I'm not sure I know . . ."

"That's Langston Hughes," I chimed in. I was starting to recognize some of the faces. "And I think that's Gertrude somebody?"

"Yes! Sasha Masha, yes . . . Stein. Gertrude Stein."

Green jumped in. "Marlon Riggs. Frank O'Hara. Alice James." He was going in rows, in stretches, faces next to each other I wouldn't have expected to be next to each other. "Keith Haring. Quentin Crisp. Constantine Cavafy."

And he started taking turns with Coco. The names came fast.

"Leslie Feinberg."

"Essex Hemphill."

"Harry Hay."

"Divine."

"Ma Rainey."

"Audre Lorde."

"Charles Ludlam."

"Christine Jorgensen."

"Agnes Martin."

"Assotto Saint."

"Hibiscus and Sylvester."

"Tim Dlugos."

"Tituba."

"Félix González-Torres."

"Bayard Rustin."

"Alberta Hunter."

"Hervé Guibert."

"May Sarton."

"Reinaldo Arenas."

"Tom Joslin."

"Bambi Lake."

Then the hall turned a corner and there were more; it seemed like we might go forever. There were names and names and faces and raised open palms, and a part of me wanted to write them all down, but I started to see that the list was endless, really.★

Andre caught my eye, then turned to Coco and said it might be time for us to head out.

"Right in the middle like that? We're just warming up."

"I know, I know," Andre said. "But it's late. Next time, okay?"

"All right. If you insist."

★ It wasn't actually endless. But it was long. There are a bunch more at the end of this book.

"Let the children go, Coco," Green said, and gave Coco's shoulder a squeeze.

"Just remember, dear," Coco said to me. "People like us, we've been here forever."

They sent us out into the night with freezer bags full of biscuits.

Chapter 18

The next two days crawled by. Andre kept sending me text messages to make sure I was free on Saturday for Miss Thing.

"u r obsessed with miss thing," I texted him.

"i am obsessed. no lie"

"what do i need to know?"

"nothing. just don't make other plans"

"what if i get an overwhelming craving to stay home and do sudoku?"

"u don't know what ur getting yrself into," he wrote, "but ur getting yrself into something big. ok?"

"ok :)," I replied.

When Tracy and I had class together, I tried to smile at her, but she just gave me a somber little nod and turned away. Then I'd remember the smell of her car or that yellow couch on a rainy day and I'd get a stabby feeling in my chest. Thankfully, there were no group projects forcing us to deal with each other more than we had to.

Soon Saturday came and it was time to head to Andre's. I buckled myself into my dad's car and turned the key. The heat came blasting on. My mind wouldn't stay still. I pulled away from the curb and into the street, into the city. Inside the car it was warm and muffled, but outside the whole autumnal world seemed sharper, somehow; the city of Baltimore seemed more vivid and more strange. It was as if my eyes were registering a change that was about to happen—but hadn't yet. I stopped at a light and noticed something bright in my peripheral vision: by the side of the road, a fox with black feet and black eyes staring out of the most gorgeous orange-red coat. For a second I thought it was looking at me. The person behind me honked. The fox ran off. It had to be a sign of something. A good omen. The city crackled with readiness for what Andre had insisted was going to be a big night.

"Sasha Masha! Come in, come in. Sorry—it's a bit of a disaster zone in here."

It was like a suitcase had exploded: there were jackets and shirts all over everything. A big dog jumped up on me and almost knocked me over. Andre told me this was Emmet and kept trying to get him to calm down.

"Just push him off, you have to push him off," he said. "Emmet! Emmet!"

I think Emmet scratched me through my shirt, and he was smelly and had drool flying everywhere, but I didn't mind. Andre grabbed my hand and pulled me down the hall. When we made it to his room, he closed the door behind us.

"Sorry," he said. "And welcome."

"Are your parents here?"

"No, my mom works late on Saturdays. But she says hi."

"Hi back," I said.

There was as much chaos in Andre's tiny room as I'd glimpsed in the living room. His bed was covered in clothes, and his closet was open with more clothes spilling out onto the floor. He had a stack of five or six books by a lamp on a table. There was an unplugged computer monitor by the door, with a bright green and orange stuffed snake draped over it. The walls were covered in band posters.

Andre had done his nails in yellow and was padding around in big slippers. He said we should figure out our looks.

"I like your nails," I said.

"Have you done yours before?"

"Not really."

"Do you want to do yours?" he asked. "Just to try?"

"Oh—sure." My heart was pounding in my chest.

"Green? Or yellow?"

"Green," I said.

He unscrewed the bottle and a sharp, acidic smell filled the room. I was already thinking about how I'd get the paint off before my parents could see. Probably there was nail polish remover in one of the drawers in our bathroom. I could just get up early Sunday morning and scrub them clean.

I pinched the brush between two fingers, and went slow, but I couldn't get the color to stay where I wanted it to. I looked at Andre's perfect canary ovals. Already I had green polish everywhere. "How do you do yours so neatly?"

"Practice. It all takes practice."

I sighed.

"Now what are we thinking as far as looks go? You didn't bring anything, did you?"

I hadn't. Looks? Was I supposed to have looks?

"That's okay." Andre was a queer on fire. Focused and set on action. "We'll find you something. I just want you to feel . . . good. Yourself. You know?"

He looked at me. I nodded.

"Now what would Sasha Masha wear?"

Andre dug through piles of clothes as I finished my nails. At my Jewish school we used to talk about the hand of God, or God guiding someone's hand toward something. Later, I was tempted to think that the universe guided Andre's hand to this dress in particular, even though I knew that it was probably chance. Or maybe just good taste. But out of all the piles of clothes in the room, he reached down and pulled up something the color of the perfect sunset. The color just before dusk. The color of air that smelled like citrus and peace and a place you never wanted to leave.

"How about this?" he asked.

"Sure," I said, my voice tiny in the back of my throat. "That'll probably work."

As I waited for my nails to dry, Andre assessed his own options clothing-wise. He held things up and dropped them, half tried on vests and jackets, and checked himself in the mirror, running through theme and variations. I didn't say anything, just watched him work.

Finally I was ready to make my way to the bathroom to try on the dress. I folded my pants and my shirt—after carefully extracting my wallet, keys, and phone—and left them in a neat pile on the toilet seat. I held up the dress to make sense of what was front and what was back, and then I slipped it over my head. The fabric landed lightly on my shoulders, hung down over my chest. The elastic waist cinched gently above my belly button, and the folds of red-orange fabric tumbled down around my legs. I could feel the hem grazing the backs of my calves.

I looked in the mirror and saw my face hovering awkwardly above the glowing ruddy neckline. I smiled at myself. I touched my arms and noticed there were goose bumps everywhere, but that was probably just because the bathroom was cold. I went back to Andre's room to get his approval. Still—and I was starting to know what it felt like to know things in your bones, your heart, your gut—in some deep part of my body I knew I looked good.

"I approve!" he said. "But you feel good? That's the most important thing, that it feels good. Does it feel good?"

I nodded. Smiled a little, even.

"What should I do with these?" I had my wallet, phone, and keys in my hand.

"Here, I'm bringing this little backpack. You can put them in here."

Andre had landed on a bright orange mesh vest over

purple-and-green quilted pants; the pant legs swung loose around his ankles. We pulled on our jackets, Andre hooked the small backpack over his shoulder, and soon we were locking the house and heading out. His canary fingernails glowed in the dusk. He told me to drive us north and east, and we bent around the harbor toward Patterson Park. Andre found the radio station that was playing the perfect song. There was a light tang of something floral that wafted off the dress I was wearing. It smelled like lilac, like late nights and sweat. An Andre smell. We drove in silence while the heat blasted and the beat of the song wrapped itself around us.

"You ready?" he asked.

"Yeah," I said, and did a little dance in the driver's seat.

A few minutes later, we were pulling up to the Lavender Ladder. Andre insisted that I wasn't going to pay for anything. "Next time we split it," he said. "But Miss Thing is its own night. It's an initiation."

Inside, the whole place had been transformed. None of the fluorescents were on; it was all twinkling, warm light with spots of color. Two round-faced teenagers with shaved heads were sitting behind a table at the entrance. Music with a heavy beat was coming from down the hall.

"Welcome to Miss Thing," said one of the teenagers behind the table. "This is a teens party, which means no alcohol, no drugs. Affirmative verbal consent is a must before any physical contact. That means anything less than 'yes' or 'hell yes' is a no. Anyone who can't keep themselves together will be asked to leave. It's five dollars to enter. Does that sound good to you, bbz?"

We both nodded, and Andre fished in his wallet for cash.

"Thank you," I muttered, unsure how to stand in my dress. I tried crossing my right leg over my left and swaying a little. I was glad the lights were low.

"I love your dress," one of the teenagers said to me, winking as we offered our wrists to get them stamped. I lowered my eyes and mustered a slight nod of acknowledgment.

The music got louder as we moved down the hall. Andre strode ahead of me. I felt the dress swishing madly against my legs as I tried to keep up. Other kids stood along the hallway in pairs and trios, drinking out of blue plastic cups. There were fishnets and platform shoes, gowns and purple velvet suits. Some people had their phones out, taking pictures of themselves in small groups; other people were taking pictures of each other. Barely anyone looked at me. The hairs on the sides of my neck were vibrating with the beat.

We passed through the double doors into the room where I'd come with Mabel, brought Tracy to see *Querelle,* first met Andre, and first said my name to a roomful of strangers. I expected a dense and sweaty crowd, but the room was mostly empty. There were maybe twenty, twenty-five people there. They were sitting in chairs around the edges, standing by the drinks table; three brave souls were swirling and prancing to the music in the center of the room. The light was dim and purple, and there were strings of beads hanging from the ceiling. Still, the beat was all around us, pressing in on our skins, holding us. Andre, as if he was reading my mind, leaned in. "It's early yet," he said. I felt his nose graze my ear. "Come."

I followed him to a cluster of chairs. We had to lean in close to each other to be heard.

"What would you like to drink? Coke? Ginger ale?"

"Um . . . Coke?"

I watched our jackets while Andre went to get us drinks. I asked someone the time. It was a little after eight. Was this going to go all night? And who were these people? I thought I recognized someone on the dance floor from the youth group meeting, but otherwise saw no one I knew. It was a weird feeling—here, in my city, the city where I'd lived for all of my seventeen years, to realize that there were whole universes of people I never knew existed.

Andre returned with two blue cups and someone he wanted me to meet.

"Sasha Masha, this is my friend Michelle. Michelle, this is Sasha Masha."

"Hi," I said, and touched her hand. "Michelle?"

"Hi Sasha Masha. I've heard about you."

Michelle was perched confidently on heels that were impressively tall. She dropped a purse on the table and lowered herself into a seat beside me.

"So how did you and Andre meet again?" she asked. I could smell strawberry perfume when she leaned in to speak into my ear.

"Oh, just sort of randomly," I said back, into hers. "We were both at one of the movie screenings here . . ."

"Cool."

"How about you?"

"Yeah, from around. We go to school together."

"Cool."

We nodded at each other. I felt myself panic a bit for lack of anything else to say.

"It's so loud here," she said. "It's hard to talk."

"It is!" I replied.

And then she started moving her mouth as if she were saying something complicated, and waving her hands around like she was talking, but no sound came out. I grinned and pumped my head up and down like I understood her perfectly. Then it was my turn, and I mouthed my own series of nonsense points, accompanied by gestures, while she made a very serious face of acknowledgment. Then we laughed and both stared out at the dance floor.

Andre leaned in to me from the other side. "Michelle is one of my best friends at school. She literally saved my life when I was a sophomore and she was a freshman."

I nodded at that, too.

Eventually Andre wanted to get up and dance. I said I'd join, but out in the middle of the room I felt stiff and exposed. I swayed and swirled the dress a little bit, but I didn't know what else to do. Andre bounced and lifted his legs and he and Michelle looked at each other and made faces. The people around me all seemed to be having a good time. Why couldn't I relax and have a good time, too?

I slipped away to the bathroom. It felt a little funny going into the men's room in a dress, but no one else was in there. I stood for a second in front of the mirror and looked at myself. What was I doing? What was this about? The door opened and someone came in. I jumped and fumbled as if to pretend that I hadn't been standing there, staring at myself. But the boy who came in just laughed and said, "Live your life, girl! You look good!" before vanishing into one of the stalls and starting to pee loudly. So I did live my life, standing there and making myself look in the mirror, really look. There was something in what I saw that I couldn't quite resolve. It was different from the look I had in the photograph with Mabel, but it went someplace equally deep. It was similar to the feeling you get when you know you know something but can't remember it. Except I knew there was nothing I was supposed to remember. It was something I felt like I should see, but wasn't seeing yet. A little tickle at the back of the eye, except it wasn't in my eye, or even my brain; it was in my heart, somehow. I didn't have a name for it. I just had "Sasha Masha."

When the boy in the stall flushed, I went into another stall myself, lifted the dress around my hips, and sat down to think. The bathroom was bright and the thudding music was a buzz that barely came through the walls. I closed my eyes and focused on the texture of the fabric against my shoulders, my back. I felt comfortable, safe. I tried to picture myself in the mirror again. "I look pretty," I said to myself. I said it again: "I look pretty." Did I look pretty? Maybe I just looked like a freak. The faucet ran and the person who'd come in to pee pumped the paper towel dispenser and ripped the paper. It got loud for a minute when he opened the door to leave, but then it closed and I was pretty sure I was alone again. It felt good to be alone. No one I knew from school or my family could see me. Knowing none of them would appear, I felt something loosen in my chest.

I figured I had come this far. I figured none of the people here would judge me, even if everyone in the rest of my life would. I figured I should probably get back out on the dance floor.

The room was much less empty than it had been. There were lots of people dancing now, bouncing and twisting and making shapes with their arms. I scanned the crowd for Andre and Michelle, and soon I saw Andre's blue hair floating above all the other heads.

"Where'd you go!" Andre wanted to know.

"I just went to the bathroom," I told him.

"Everything okay?" he asked, smiling, and I nodded.

Michelle touched my arm. "We thought we'd lost you!"

It was easier to dance in the crowd. I loosened my knees and let the beat into my hips. The room was warm from all the sweating bodies, and the smell of the dress, Andre's smell, found its way to my nose. I kept my eyes down, but I could tell I was starting to vibrate with all the people around me. I watched Michelle's feet and Andre's feet step in and away, I watched the patterns of all the feet around us, stepping forward and back, side to side, always in pairs, first one, then the other. A smile was playing across my face, but maybe no one saw it. The music had made it into my body and my body was loose, even if I didn't know what to do with my hands, my hands probably looked stupid, but at least my feet knew what to do, and the music was in my body and my body felt good. I watched the fabric sunset swish and wrap itself around my ankles, I watched my legs appear and disappear in the cloth.

Andre went away for a bit and then came back with a bottle of water, which he shared with me and Michelle. We passed it around and made mute smiles at each other. The music wrapped around us like a knitted rug, slow ripples and rises and deep, dark folds. I liked being here. I raised my hands up to the ceiling and followed them with my gaze, I watched the light reflecting off all the beads suspended above us. I lowered my arms and my eyes and started to take in all the faces around me. There were soft faces and sharp faces, round faces and long ones, faces made up with dusky reds or powder blues, there was acne and flush throbbing dully under makeup and glitter. A few of the faces regarded mine and smiled at me. Andre's face was a moon I wanted to keep close by; Michelle's was another friendly planet. All around me, this galaxy, rotating and expanding. The music kept us all in orbit, kept us all breathing. I wondered how long we'd been here. It suddenly felt like forever.

Andre leaned in close. "Wanna go outside and get some fresh air?"

I nodded and looked at Michelle, who nodded, too, and we all threaded our way through the crowd and toward the exit.

The cold air of the street hit my face like water, filled my lungs until they tingled. We sighed and stumbled out onto the sidewalk, then leaned together by the wall. I felt my goose-bump-speckled shoulder press against Michelle's. Her skin was warm.

"Not so bad, eh, Sasha Masha?" Andre was saying, as he stretched his long arms straight up in the air. "Are you having fun?"

I nodded. I didn't want to break the spell with the sound of my voice.

"Yeah, it's a pretty magical night," he said. "When you said you were starting to come out, especially, I was like, *Yes! Perfect timing! Sasha Masha needs to come to Miss Thing.*"

"It happens every year?"

Andre nodded. "This is my third year coming."

A light must have changed, because cars came streaming down the street. Someone honked—it might have been at us. I watched the traffic but with a far-off squint in my eye. Just a river of red and white light. I looked back at Andre.

"Was that before or after your *zhush*?" I asked quietly, and pressed my lips together against the cold.

"My what?"

"Your—didn't you say like two years ago, you had a . . ."

"Ohhh!! My *zhush*. Lol. Yes. I can't believe you remember that." He laughed. "I'm so stupid sometimes." He shuffled his feet and looked at the pavement. "No, that was after. That was just after, I think. You were there with me, weren't you, Michelle?"

"I was, I was. I had just started to transition. I don't think I was . . . or I think I was still pretty early along."

My breath caught in my throat just a second. I stared at my feet and kicked the pavement, but I wanted to look at Michelle again. Was Michelle trans? I didn't think I'd met a trans person before. Her shoulder was still pressed against mine, and her skin was still warm.

"Two years then for you, too, no?"

"Two years, baby."

"All right, I'm cold," Andre said. "I'm going inside."

Michelle and I followed. We flashed our wrists to the bored-looking person at the door. Andre led the way and I picked up the rear. I watched Michelle's back, the back of her neck. She had wonderful posture.

In the main room, Andre and Michelle found someone named Timmy, and everyone hugged and kissed each other on the cheeks and I got introduced and cheeks brushed and bodies got jostled and we all threaded our way into the dancing crowd. The room was warmer, the bodies closer together. I kept trying to steal glances at Michelle. I wanted to read her history in her face. I couldn't stop looking at her. If anything, knowing she was trans made me think she was even more beautiful.

Timmy was a better dancer than anyone else: he took up space and everyone wanted to watch him move. I watched Andre watch him; I watched his face glow with appreciation. I saw the way he could meet the eyes of a stranger, too, and the way his face would twitch with mischief and invitation and warmth. Andre was magic like that. His whole body seemed light and loose and open, and I felt lucky to have a crush on someone so well-liked, someone who called me by my stupid name, and who wanted to have me around. But then I felt a wave of melancholy, that blue shadow, fall from my head down to my feet. My body was tired. I dragged myself behind the beat and my legs felt heavy. I told Andre in his ear that I was gonna take a little break and made my way toward the door. Why did this sadness have to come back every time I started to get happy?

What time was it? My phone was in Andre's bag. I guess I could have asked one of the people lingering out in the hall—a few people were slumped against the wall, leaning their heads back and closing their eyes— but I was a little bit dizzy and just wanted to go somewhere I could close a door and not be seen.

In the bathroom, someone was hunched over the sink with the water running, but all the stalls were open. I took the farthest one, latched the door behind me, hoisted my dress, and slouched onto the toilet. The water ran a little while longer but then it stopped, and after a moment or two more I heard the person leave.

My head drooped and dangled. I could see down the front of my dress to the soft curve of my belly and the elastic band of my boxers. I looked at my green nails and my chapped and clumsy fingers. I shivered.

Could I be trans? Could that be what the whole Sasha Masha thing was about?

The thought seemed ridiculous at first. That wasn't

a word I'd ever thought about applying to myself. I was a boy, a clumsy, pudgy, soft-spoken boy, a boy who smiled and everyone liked. But something was wrong. There was a high wall inside of me, and it made me angry, it made me stuck; there was a self on the other side—was this, now, the thing I'd failed to see? That in my heart of hearts I wasn't a boy after all? I closed my eyes and tried to imagine my boy-body melting away and leaving the body of a girl. As I did, I felt my breath drop down deeper into my belly, I felt my heart slow and the muscles that clenched my ribs together go slack. I thought about that feeling of a creature who wanted to run around inside me, a creature who I mostly kept locked away in a room.

Was that it? Could that be it?

I wasn't sure I *wanted* that to be it.

A part of me wanted to go back home to the house I'd never liked, strip off this dress, and crawl into my bed. Finally give in and let that house wrap me up inside it, stay forever in familiar blankets and a dark room. What was I doing here? Who was I, with this nail polish, this dress?

Someone else came into the bathroom. I stood up quickly, flushed the toilet, and lurched back out into the hall. The music was still going, a different beat now, a different key, but the same thick carpet of music. I went to look for Andre and Michelle, tell them I should probably go home. The dress felt stupid. I felt like a stupid freak. What time was it, anyway?

I felt Andre's hand on my arm before I saw him.

"We want to go get pizza," Andre said into my ear. "Do you want to go get pizza?"

I looked up and saw Andre, Michelle, and Timmy. My eyes met Michelle's. She smiled and looked back at me. My heart sped up.

"Sure," I said. "Let's get pizza."

Chapter 19

~~~~~~~~~~

The four of us staggered out onto the sidewalk in a bit of a daze. The air was cold and raw. Michelle was limping in her high heels, and Timmy kept sighing. I led the way to the car. We all piled in without a word. The clock lit up and said it was ten forty-five. So it was late, but not too late. Andre handed me my phone, and I looked to see if I had any messages.

My mom had texted: "Just checking on you. You having a good time?"

"Yah," I texted back. "Just hanging out. I'll be home soon."

She replied right away. "Sounds good, sweetie." And sent a heart.

"Onward!" Timmy crowed from the back seat.

Andre turned to me. "Do you know where we're going?"

"Nope," I said, "no idea." I handed him my phone.

"Great," he replied, laughing. "I'll navigate."

Michelle had slumped over onto Timmy's shoulder. I could see her face, relaxed, resting, in the rearview mirror. Her eyes twitched under their gently closed lids. Timmy was closing his eyes, too, and had rested a hand on Michelle's knee. I pulled out into traffic, and once Andre had given me my first set of directions, all four of us fell into silence. It didn't feel bad. It felt exhausted. It felt comfortable. It felt happy. Andre's phone dinged with a text message, and his attention disappeared into the screen. I watched the road. I'd driven these streets many times before, but almost always by myself, or with my parents. Maybe once or twice with Tracy. Now I was the one steering this ship, and I had these three passengers in my care. Two seemed to be sleeping and one was in another world, in his phone. I sat up in my seat a little bit, held my arms a little more lightly. If only for a moment, it felt equal parts lonely and lovely to be the captain of a ship. *The lady captain,* I thought, trying it on.

"Are we there yet?" Timmy blurted with his eyes closed.

"Hush, Timmy," Michelle said, tapping his arm.

"Fuck, sorry, Sasha Masha," Andre said. "I stopped paying attention. It's just up here, on the right."

Soon we'd parked and were making our way up the street.

Timmy and Michelle were discussing what kind of slices exactly they were going to get. Andre walked beside me.

"I just want you to know," he said, and threaded his arm in mine, "that I think you look quite beautiful in that dress."

"Well, thank you," I managed to say. But after that it was like my words were gone, and not in a bad way. In a way where I didn't need to say anything at all. All I needed to do was walk arm in arm with Andre. We passed a gas station and a fast-food place. We passed a nail salon with a metal grate pulled across the entrance. A car with a rattling engine roared nearby and startled us all. The streetlights buzzed and something smelled off. But still, somehow, just now, the world seemed absolutely perfect. The blue shadow was banished again. Maybe I'd left it back at the party.

Ordering our slices of pizza proved quite a complicated deliberation. Timmy kept changing his mind, though he knew he wanted something with pineapple, and Andre kept trying to order for him. Everything Michelle asked for they didn't have. By the time we had settled at a table and they hollered that our pizza was ready, I was ravenous. We hunkered down, each of us daubing greasy cheese with square white napkins.

"Let this pizza be known throughout the ages as holy pizza," Timmy said.

"Holy pizza," Michelle echoed.

"Because lo it came unto us when we were tired."

"Tired."

"And hungry."

"Hungry."

"And thereupon we ate the pizza," Timmy concluded, chewing. He swallowed. "And it was good."

"Oh, my dear ones," Andre said, leaning back in his chair, wiping his mouth. "I'm so glad to be surrounded by your beautiful faces."

He sighed and for a while we just chewed, staring off into space, while late-night radio commercials dribbled out of ceiling speakers.

"I'd like to propose," Michelle said, pushing away her greasy paper plate, "that we make a pact. An eternal pact. Forged here, tonight, over this pizza."

"And what's the pact?"

"That we will always remember, no matter how dark it gets, that we don't have to face the darkness alone. We can always ask for help. Nobody actually does it alone. Everybody needs somebody."

"*Everybody needs somebody . . . ,*" Timmy started to sing.

"Are we agreed?"

"I'm in," Andre said.

"I'm in," Timmy echoed, through a mouthful of pizza.

"Sasha Masha?" Michelle said. "I may have just met you, but you're here. You're having pizza. Are you in?"

I swallowed. I wiped my mouth with the one clean corner of my crumpled napkin.

"Yeah," I said. "I'm in."

Just then I started to hear some laughter coming from behind me. I wouldn't have noticed if it hadn't been for the weird silence that settled quickly around it. I looked over and saw that it was two men in their thirties, probably. They were wearing suit jackets and both were leaning heavily against the counter. They might have been drunk. They were looking at me.

I quickly turned back around.

"You see that?" I heard one of them say to the other.

"I do," the other said, and chuckled.

"That is a grown-ass boy. In a dress."

And they both started cackling again.

Everyone around our table had gotten quiet. I caught Andre's eye, and he shook his head ever so slightly, like, *don't engage with them.*

"You don't see that every day, do you? That's some funny shit."

They kept chuckling. I could hear their bodies shift against the counter. All of a sudden Timmy stood up and turned toward them.

"*Timmy!*" Andre hissed.

"Can I ask," he said, in a controlled voice, "that you not talk that way about my friend?"

They didn't say anything. They just started chuckling louder. I wanted to disappear. I felt ashamed. I felt stupid. I felt like a child. I wished I'd stayed home. I wished I'd never thought of the name Sasha Masha. I wished I could be a Real boy, a careless boy, the kind of boy who sprawled on couches and guffawed nastily and made other people anxious.

Out of the corner of my eye, I saw Timmy take a step closer. "It's not respectful."

That made them laugh even louder.

"Miss! Miss!" one of them said, in a mocking, nasal voice. The other one hooted with laughter.

I couldn't move. Suddenly I was scared. I could picture one of them picking me up and throwing me to the floor. I could picture either of them doing the same to Andre and Timmy and Michelle.

"Hey!" Timmy said, his voice edging toward a shout. "I'm talking to you!"

"Timmy, we're going," Andre said, standing, grabbing Timmy by the arm and pulling him toward the door. Michelle put her arm around me and we followed, leaving our table littered with napkins and unfinished pieces of pizza. As Michelle and I hustled down the block after Andre and Timmy, I caught a glimpse of the two men inside, cracking up.

"How am I gonna let them talk like that?" I heard Timmy saying.

"Timmy, they were drunk and they were assholes," Andre replied. "I have no interest in starting a fight. We're going home."

"It fucking sucks!"

"I know."

Michelle was holding me close as we walked. "You all right?" she asked.

I shrugged, but my heart was racing. I felt flustered and weak. "I guess so."

"It does fucking suck," she said. "I still get that sometimes, too. You know not to take it seriously, but it sucks."

"Yeah," I said. But some part of me believed that what they said was true: that I was just a boy in a dress, and that a boy in a dress was a pathetic, worthless thing.

We gathered once we'd made it a couple of blocks away and stood there in a cozy huddle. Andre asked if I was okay, and Timmy said he wanted to punch those motherfuckers in the face.

"All right, honey," Andre said to that. "I don't know if I've ever seen you manage to kill a fly, so I'm not too convinced . . ."

"Psshhhh . . ."

"No kung fu fantasias, okay? Is that a deal? Part of the pizza club deal or whatever?"

It felt good to laugh a little. It felt good to stand together in a circle, holding each other.

After we'd dropped Timmy and Michelle back off at their cars, we headed to Andre's house. The heat was on, and the streets were empty. It was sleepy and quiet.

"Thanks for having me along," I said. "This was really . . . special."

"Of course, Sasha Masha. I'm so glad you came. I'm just sorry it ended that way."

"It's okay. It happens."

"It does happen. And it is never fun. But it's also not everything."

We drove quietly a minute and listened to the hum of the engine and the stillness of the city.

"I don't know." I took a deep breath. "I'd never worn a dress out in public before."

"How does it feel?"

"It feels good. It feels right, somehow."

Andre didn't say anything for a minute.

"Is it weird if I say . . . ," he began. "Just, when I met you, I felt that there was something about you . . . And it took me a while to even articulate what it was consciously. But I think what I sensed was something like, Oh, here's a person who has a really beautiful feminine part of their soul. And maybe hasn't brought it into the world yet."

"Yeah," I said. I thought a moment. "Maybe. Maybe that's true."

"Did you ever think about trying different pronouns, or . . . ?"

"Not really," I said quickly. "But maybe. I don't know. Maybe."

"What pronouns feel good? What pronouns would you like me to use?"

"Um, I don't know. I think I'm all right with just the regular."

"What's the regular? Is there a regular?"

"I mean, he, him. Yeah."

"Okay. Sure." Andre looked over at me. "Well, if you ever change your mind, just let me know."

"I will," I said. "Thanks."

Eventually we pulled up in front of his house. We sat for a moment in the car as the engine settled down, let off heat, clicked a few times.

"Well, thanks, Sasha Masha," Andre said. "This was a really nice night."

"Um. I guess I have to get my stuff from your bag. Could I come in with you to change?"

"Oh! Duh! Sorry, Sasha Masha."

I followed him up the walkway. It was cold, my legs were cold. He unlocked the door and I followed as quietly as I could into the dim inside.

"*My mom's probably sleeping, so . . . shhh . . .*"

"*Of course,*" I whispered.

We moved without talking. He turned on the bathroom light for me and indicated that he'd be in his room. My pants and shirt had been moved to the edge of the tub. Gingerly, I lifted the dress up and over my shoulders, then folded it delicately and placed it beside my boy clothes. I looked at my pale, lumpy body in the mirror. Was there actually a feminine part of my soul? And if there was, how did I get to it? I shook my jeans out and pulled them up and over my legs. I tugged my shirt over my head and slipped my arms through the sleeves. In the mirror I saw the Alex I recognized. I wondered if I could start to see that Alex differently.

Back in his room, Andre had changed into sweatpants and a T-shirt. He was cramming a pile of clothes into the closet.

"Well," I said. "Thanks again."

"Oh! Of course," he said, and closed the door

behind me. "Sorry, I just don't want to *make too much noise*," he added in a whisper.

"Oh! Yeah, definitely."

"You had a good time?"

"I had a really good time."

"If you'd like, you can keep the dress."

"Oh! No, I don't have to . . ."

"As you may have noticed, I have a lot of clothes. And it fits you better than it fits me." He shrugged, and his face twitched into a winning grin. "So."

"Okay," I said. "I think I will."

"Good."

"I think my wallet and things are still in your . . ."

"Oh! Yes yes yes." He turned toward the bed to rummage through his backpack.

I knew it was probably pretty late. But I didn't want to look at my phone yet. I wasn't ready to leave. Then Andre had my wallet, phone, and keys in his outstretched hands. He held them for me as I fit them, one by one, into my jeans pockets.

"You got them all?"

"Yeah," I said. My heart was racing.

"Excellent."

"Um," I began, "would it be all right if I—"

And I didn't finish the sentence, because I knew if I waited any longer I'd persuade myself not to do what I was about to do, which was to step forward, lurch, really, place a shaking hand awkwardly on Andre's arm, and lean in and up toward his face, where I landed my chilly, trembling lips on his.

Our mouths touched for just a second—long enough for me to feel the warm tension of his narrow lips—and then he placed a hand on my chest and stepped back.

"Oh, sorry, hey."

I immediately blushed all over and wanted to be a million miles away. What was maybe a little comforting was that Andre seemed completely flustered, too, in a way I'd never seen him before. He looked everywhere but at me, walked in a little circle, and landed sitting on his bed.

"Sorry. I'm really sorry," I said. And I could feel my heart speeding up with the fear that I'd broken something I wouldn't be able to put back together. "That was really dumb."

"No, it's—you just didn't give me much warning."

"I'm really sorry."

"You didn't even finish the question. You were asking and you didn't even finish."

"I know, I'm really . . . I'm so sorry, Andre."

"It's—sorry, no, that was harsher than I meant it to be. Can we just—hold on."

"I can go."

"No! No. It's very . . . I like you very much, Sasha Masha, and I'm very flattered, but actually Timmy and I—"

"Oh." I almost didn't want to hear the rest of the sentence. *Why am I so stupid? Stupid, stupid, stupid. Never again will I do anything like that ever.* I only paid attention to snippets of what Andre said next, but that was enough.

". . . a long time since we were a real thing . . . off and on for a little bit . . . give it another go . . . the whole monogamy thing . . ."

I nodded a bunch. He swallowed and looked at my face. "Sorry. I hope I wasn't giving confusing signals."

"No, it's . . ." I had no idea what was and wasn't

true anymore about the last few weeks. Maybe I was just fated to be alone for the rest of my life. Dumb and awkward and itchy and alone. I was stupid and a freak and I should just go home and hide and be Alex for the rest of my life.

"I think you're so great, and so . . . beautiful, Sasha Masha. And I just think figuring out who you are and who you want to be can be so hard when you don't have friends who get it. And there was this kid who was really important to me when I was coming out, and I guess I thought . . . I don't know. I wanted to be able to do for you what he did for me. But I guess I made kind of a mess of it all."

"No, it's okay," I said. "I'm just really sorry. Um. I have to go home."

"Okay. Well, get some rest and text me tomorrow, okay? We can—"

But I was already out the door.

So much for a pact. Stupid pact.

In the car I pulled out my phone. 1:43. Fuck. I had two missed calls from my mom and four from my dad.

There were text messages, too:

"Alex it's getting late."

"Alex where are you?"

"Pls call one of us thx."

"Helloo?"

My hands were trembling so much I could barely type, but I texted a quick, "Sorry coming home," remembered to turn on the headlights, and shifted into gear. A hard, digital female voice led me back to familiar streets. I was shaking the whole time.

When I got inside, the house was dark. They'd gone upstairs to sleep, which was almost more frightening than their being downstairs, awake and upset.

"Alex?" The quiet voice of my mom came through the partially open door as I creaked up the stairs.

"Yeah," I said.

No answer.

The clock in my room said 2:34 when I had finally brushed my teeth, undressed, and slipped into bed. I played through images of the night, conversations, faces, feelings. I thought about the way things ended in the pizza parlor, but then I pushed back to what had happened before. I thought about the entryway, and the teenager who stamped my wrist, and the dance floor, and the bathroom. I thought about pineapple pizza and greasy napkins and I thought about the pact. I thought again about kissing—trying to kiss—Andre, and shuddered. I thought about what I didn't know of Andre and Timmy's history together. I thought about what I didn't know about Andre. And I thought about what I didn't know about myself.

The last thing I remember thinking about before I drifted off was that red-orange dress, like a sunset, like a dream. I came so close, and then I fucked it all up. I heard the men's laughter in the pizza parlor and I heard the phrase *grown-ass boy in a dress*. Then I remembered. The dress was just where I'd left it: folded carefully on the edge of the bathtub, back in Andre's house.

Chapter 20

Early the next morning Murphy was scratching at the underside of my door like nothing had changed.

Oh, Murphy. Dear Murphy.

I wish you'd let me sleep.

I dragged a pillow over my head. *Scratch. Scratch. Scratch.* Finally I got out of bed, shuffled downstairs to the kitchen, opened a new can of cat food, and scooped half into a bowl. I stood there, leaning against the doorway, and watched Murphy eat. My eyes were starting to open. He ate with focus and determination. I could hear his little tongue and lips clicking and smacking the puree. There were sounds from upstairs. So my parents were just getting up, too. I caught a glimpse of my hands and my green nail polish. The whole night before came flooding back. I turned to dash upstairs so I could get rid of the color, but my mom was already coming down. She was in her pajamas.

"That was bad, Alex. That was really, really bad."

"I know. I'm sorry."

I shoved my hands into the pockets of my gym shorts.

"Your dad's still sleeping. I don't think either of us got much rest last night. We talked a lot, trying to figure out . . . You've never . . . we've never had to punish you before. But this was . . ." She shook her head. "This was bad, Alex." She looked at me. "I sort of can't believe you. What happened?"

"I don't know."

"What is going on, that all of a sudden you act like this?"

"Mom, I just—"

"You're, like, grounded. You're really, really grounded."

"Yeah," I said, and flopped down on the couch, keeping my hands in my pockets.

"I'm sorry. I didn't let you finish. But I just don't understand what's going on. Who is this Andrew person? Where were you?"

"He's a friend, Mom. He's a new friend."

"What are you doing together until two in the morning? Are you getting high?"

"No!"

"I'm sorry to be crude about it, but I'm just trying to get a complete picture!"

"Mom, no, he's a new friend. I lost track of time. And then I had to give people rides."

"So you're a taxi driver now? None of these people can get home themselves? Were people drinking, Alex? You're lucky you didn't get pulled over."

"No, nobody was drinking, I said I lost track of time."

"Do you need me to get you a watch? Would that help? I don't know how you lose track of time for two whole hours. Fifteen, twenty minutes, maybe, but—where was your phone? We texted you a million times!"

My dad came down with messy hair.

"What the hell were you thinking?" he asked.

"I'm sorry, I lost track of time."

"That's not how this works, Alex! When you say you're going to be home at a certain time—"

"I told him," my mom muttered.

"If you say that, then you create expectations, and then to just not reply, to not communicate—"

"I'm not on my phone all the time, Dad, in spite of what people your age like to think about people my age. Sometimes I'm paying attention to other things. I'm really sorry, but—"

"Okay, but you don't get to just *not pay attention* when we expect you home and suddenly it's two in the morning and we have no idea where the hell you are!"

"Okay! I heard you!"

"You, my friend, are grounded."

"I told him," my mom muttered again.

"You are very, very grounded."

* * *

I lay on my bed.

A howl tore through my body and I slammed my fist into the blanket. Then I started to cry. I was crying because I felt like I'd lost something. Everything, maybe. A week ago I got a glimpse of something wonderful, and now it was gone. I was crying because I was afraid of what I would do with myself, who I would be, how I would love anybody. I was crying because of the guys at the pizza counter. I was crying because of what my parents would say. I was crying about Andre, too, tears of frustration and embarrassment.

Why had I been such an idiot? My one shot at a new friend, and I'd turned it into a fantasy of a *boy*friend. I wanted to peel my face off and die under a log. Why did I always have to mess things up like that? Why did I always have to get things wrong?

I couldn't go on like this anymore. The last week had been intense and revealed a lot. But this wasn't just about last week. The stuff that had started to surface went deep. Into the past and the darkest, most secret parts of myself. I had opened a door and the light had come in. However scared I was, I couldn't ever close that door again.

When the tears slowed down, I pulled out my phone.

"How do I know if I'm trans?" I asked the internet.

You might be trans if you've never identified with the gender you were given at birth. You might be trans if you've never felt at home in your body. Think about how you feel when people use your assigned pronouns to refer to you, or about how you feel when you behave in ways that seem expected of someone of your gender. Does it feel like you're faking it?

I'd always told myself my body was like a bad, bulky costume. Now that I thought about it this way, I did feel like I was faking it, yes.

Some trans people describe knowing from a very early age that their true gender was different from their assigned gender. But that's not true for everyone. Some people only begin to feel that way during puberty, or even later in life. Some trans people feel very clearly that they were born into one gender, and want to live as the other. But gender is a spectrum, and there are a lot of places along that spectrum where you could fall. You have to explore and see what feels right for you.

I skimmed a little more, let my eyes hop from paragraph to paragraph, from bold text to italic; there were glossaries and videos. I opened links in new tabs and flipped between them on the small rectangular screen. The prospect of answering all these questions here, now, right away, felt overwhelming. But I felt the chilly, unmistakable sense that this was exactly what I'd been experiencing most of my life.

Just then I got a text from Andre.

"Hey Sasha Masha"

My stomach dropped and I started to panic.

"Just wanted to say that I'm sorry if things got weird last night"

"I had a nice time hanging out, and if u wanna do it again as friends I'm very down"

He was typing something else—the three little dots were scrolling.

Then he wasn't typing anything.

I stared at the screen a moment.

I deleted his contact and blocked the number. I

threw my phone down on the bed. Murphy came and scratched at the door, but I didn't want to be around anybody. I wanted to stay in this bed forever. I started to cry again. Then I got tired of crying and just lay still.

I don't know how long I lay there. The sounds of the house crept into the room around me. The easy creaks and pops of wooden beams expanding and contracting. I heard my mom's voice rising through the floor, and then my dad's, both softened to a murmur. The rattle of dishes in the sink and the sound of water rushing through the pipes. Outside, the voices of two women came closer and then moved off. Birds, dogs, traffic. There was so much going on, always. Nearby and far away. The longer I listened, the more I heard. I heard the door open and close, and the car driving off. I heard Murphy scratching in his litter. I heard the electricity coursing through the walls of our house. I even heard the blood pumping through my veins.

I got out of bed and went downstairs to find a snack. The house was empty. I stood in front of the refrigerator.

I could only imagine how much my body had been trying to tell me all these years. About who I was, what clothes I wanted to wear, how I wanted to move through the world, how I saw myself, how I saw others. I never stayed still enough to listen.

I pulled out a jar of pickles and sat at the kitchen table.

Now it was like the shapes and scribbles and shadows of a murky past started to shift and slide and arrange themselves into a pattern I could recognize.

I remembered the game I used to play with Ted Goldstein in fourth grade where he was a criminal mastermind and I was his assistant, Mara. I always pictured Mara in black leather pants and a ponytail.

I remembered the story I wrote in middle school that ended with the main character saying, *I'm just an ordinary gal, don't mind me, hahaha!*

I remembered the picture I kept in a frame on my desk—not of me and Mabel, or me and my family—but of me and a drag queen who performed at the restaurant where Mabel had her sixteenth birthday party.

I remembered the hope I always harbored, when there was a school play, of "having" to play a girl, "having" to wear a dress and a wig.

All these years I'd never put the pieces together. They pointed to something that hadn't made sense to me. I hid them in different corners of my memory, where I wouldn't accidentally see them together and understand. But when I wasn't looking, they'd banded together and given themselves a name.

Sasha Masha, they said. *That's us.*

I woke up in the dark. The sound of a key in the door. For a second I wasn't sure where I was. Murphy was whining for dinner. I had a headache. Someone switched a light on in the hall and I squeezed my eyes shut. I'd fallen asleep in the living room. A person plopped down on the end of the couch by my feet and laid a hand on my leg. I muttered something.

Slowly, I opened my eyes.

"You catching up on some rest?"

It was my dad.

"Yeah," I said. "I guess."

"All right, kiddo. I'll let you get yourself together."

Through the trees outside the living room window, I could see the last purple light of day.

I had a missed call from Mabel.

I lay still with my eyes closed in the hopes that I could get this headache to go away. Someone was making dinner and had turned on the news. I remembered the feeling of being six years old and sick and curled up on the couch. I wanted to be a kid like that again.

Eventually it was time for dinner.

"It's nice to have you home, Alex," my mom said.

"It is indeed," my dad agreed. "Maybe we can watch a movie tonight?"

"Sure," I said, in a small voice.

"Is there anything you're in the mood for, sweetie?"

Why were they being so nice? It was almost like they were extra nice to me now that they had had to punish me. I said I wasn't sure. I said I'd watch anything. I set the table and brought out the big bowl of salad.

I didn't care anymore whether they saw my painted nails but if they did, they didn't say anything. My dad brought out the chicken.

"So, Alex," my mom began, "we're just a little worried about you. We're worried something's going on. Between these late nights, and the new friends, and the questions you were asking. We don't know what it is, but we want you to know that we're here for you. And we can talk about it, if you want to." She looked to my dad for confirmation.

"Yeah, kiddo. Just talk to us. We're not perfect, but we do our best."

"Mostly we just want you to be safe. You know? And we're a little worried."

I looked into both of their faces. And their faces were full of love. And I knew that I would try to explain to them.

But right now I was just too tired.

"I . . . appreciate it," I said. "And . . . I think I'm just feeling a little overwhelmed today. Can we talk about it tomorrow? Would that be okay? I promise we can talk about it. I just can't talk about it right now . . ." And as

I was starting to say those last words, tears crowded my eyes. Before I knew it, I was sobbing. Soon I was on the couch and my mom was beside me and my dad was getting toilet paper because my nose was running like crazy. I cried and cried and ugly cried and my mom hugged me and I just kept crying.

Chapter 21

~~~~~~~~

Monday morning I felt empty. Not in a bad way. It was like a huge wind had passed through my body and cleared everything away. I didn't feel happy or sad, just relieved. There are any number of metaphors for it. A storm had passed. I had crossed a threshold. Suddenly I wasn't in a rush to tell everyone I knew about Sasha Masha, because I woke up knowing that Sasha Masha was me. Simple as that.

At lunch Jake proposed that we hang out sometime outside of school. *Of course*, was my feeling, and "Of course," was what I said. But then I had to explain about the party on Saturday and how I'd stayed out late and my parents had grounded me for the next month.

"Damn, Shapelsky. I didn't know you were such a party animal," he said.

"I'm not usually," I muttered.

"Well," he said, "we'll hang out once you're un-grounded. It's all good."

I could sense some hurt in his voice. I had said I'd invite him to meet other queers, after all. Why hadn't I invited him to Miss Thing? Had I not wanted him there? That wasn't it. I genuinely liked Jake, now that we'd been hanging out again. Because of my crush on Andre? Because I was nervous to be out as Sasha Masha? Those were all *sorts* of reasons, but they weren't particularly good ones.

The best way of saying what happened might be that my heart flinched. Contracted. Withdrew itself just a little bit.

"Hey," I said. "I'm sorry I didn't invite you along on Saturday. I don't know what I was thinking. But I should have."

Jake looked at me, studied my face. "It's all right, Shapelsky," he said, though I could tell I was right to think he was hurt. "Next time."

My heart felt clear and open now. I didn't want to flinch anymore.

Last period, in chemistry, I daydreamed. I stared out the window at the tops of the trees and the buildings down the hill. When the sky was clear, you could almost see down to the harbor, where the little sailboats darted in and out around the edges and the big tankers came through from other parts of the world. I thought about our little school in the wide spread of Baltimore, and I thought about what Dr. Royce had said the first day of this year, about the school as a microcosm for the world. We should treat each other with respect, he said, and step up to the plate. *Step up to the plate.* Chemistry was on the second floor, so above us and below us were hundreds of stressed teenagers spinning in the circles of their own lives, trying to do okay and not feel too desperate or alone.

I looked over at Tracy. I wondered if she might ever agree to walk with me again by Lake Roland. Despite everything, there had been a lot of good between us, I thought. But I'd kept swallowing my feelings, and she got tired of my silence. Maybe one day I'd find a way to apologize.

She must have felt my gaze. Because just then she turned and our eyes met. Her lips pressed against each other slightly. Was it a smile? Not quite. It was something. I smiled just the littlest bit—not too much. We held our gaze for a few moments. She was the first to look away.

Mess, mess, I'd made many messes.

When the last bell rang, I decided to walk home instead of taking the bus. I wanted to be outside. I wanted to feel the chill air and watch the sky change. So I turned down Thirty-Third Street and into the sinking sun.

I also wanted to call Mabel.

She picked up right away. "I feel like I'm high," she said.

"Are you high?"

"No, Sasha Masha. I'm in love."

"Oh," I said. "That's good. With Alice?"

"Of course with Alice! Who else?" And she launched into the story of her Saturday-night date with Alice at a bowling alley. "And so we're bowling, we've got the shoes and everything, and it's my turn, and I've been telling myself I want to ask her if we can kiss, just been telling myself this over and over, and I decide that if I get at least five pins this time I'm going to do it, I'm going to ask her. So I just like fling it, like totally out of control, just sort of *the hell with this*, and it goes straight down the lane and in one swift, clean blow . . . perfect strike."

"So you kissed her??"

"Wait for it. And this was like, capital smoothness, just, like, movie-star-dyke class act, I turned on the heel of my bowling shoe and sort of strolled up to where Alice was watching, and I extended a hand, and I said, 'I'd like to kiss you, if that's all right, Alice,' and she laughed and said yes. And so then yeah. I kissed her."

"Oh, Mabel!" I said, shouting it a little in the middle of the sidewalk.

"And it was just . . . I don't know. I have no words."
She let out a noisy sigh. And then I let out a noisy sigh. And then she did and I did and for a bit there we were growling and moaning like the creatures we were. Then we laughed.

"How are you?" she asked.

As I walked, I told her all about the party on Saturday. And Andre and Timmy and Michelle. And the pizza parlor. And my stupid move at Andre's house. And my angry parents. And my day at home. And my snotty tears that wouldn't stop after dinner. And I told her that all that crying had done me good. I had woken up clearer, and emptier. I felt like something had shifted, somehow, for the better. I told her that my heart was lighter.

"Oh, Sasha Masha," she said, "I'm so happy for you."

"Can I tell you this weird theory I have?"

"Of course."

"So at the beginning of the year," I began, "Dr. Royce gave his big speech and said this thing about stepping up to the plate. And I've been thinking about what that means. Because there's a part of me that thought this whole worry about who I am was selfish or narcissistic or whatever. So I've been thinking, what does that mean, really? To step up to the plate?"

I was passing the field where my dad used to take me to kick around a soccer ball. There were two kids running up and down the length of it now, and their mom was shouting one of their names.

"I think we've each got a mystery inside of us," I said, "and as people, our job is to respect that mystery. To give it room to breathe. To feed it. To take it out for lunch sometimes. Whatever. We're all part of a whole big picture. And if we're not doing our best to unfold the strange somethings inside of us, we're not doing right by everybody else. If we're not unfolding our hearts, we're holding them back. We're flinching. And that's how we hurt people. That's how we make ourselves and the whole world smaller."

"Is that it?"

"That's it."

"That's beautiful, Sasha Masha. I love it."

By then I was basically home. Mabel told me I was

a smart cookie and she was really proud of me and she loved me. I told her I loved her, too, and was really excited about things with Alice.

As I approached the house, I saw a small brown paper package on the front stoop. I said goodbye to Mabel and brought it inside. *For SM,* it said. *You got this.*

I unwrapped the package and inside was the dress.

Chapter 22

~~~~~~~~~~~~

I unlocked the door, went right upstairs to my parents' room, and in front of my mom's floor-length mirror, I put it on. I stood there and twirled in it; tried to see how it looked from behind, over my own shoulder. I even dug around in my mom's makeup drawer and found a shade of lipstick that matched it perfectly. It made my lips shiny and sticky and smelled like the inside of her purse.

For a minute or two I just looked at myself. My face in the mirror was still my face. But it seemed right now. And it wasn't the lipstick, necessarily, or even the way the neckline of the dress framed my throat. There was a twinkle behind the eyes that made all the difference. There was a smile behind my lips and a glow behind my cheekbones. I saw a different face inside my face, even though of course it was the face I'd always had.

I went back downstairs to the living room that always made me itch and sat on the couch I'd spent so many years hating. I smoothed the dress over my thighs and watched Murphy doze in the last patch of golden light on the carpet.

I felt calm and happy all of a sudden. What was happening to me?

I laughed a little, and Murphy looked up at me. Murphy didn't care about Sasha Masha. Murphy ate and slept and enjoyed getting his head rubbed. Murphy had known about Sasha Masha all along.

Maybe, I thought, there was no such thing as a not-Real person. There was no such thing as a Real person, either. The world was Real. This couch was Real, Murphy was Real, the light and the bookshelves and the creatures and the sounds of the city moving around me—they were all Real. Like it or not, the world is Real, and whoever we are, we are part of the world.

I used to roll my eyes at stories about teenagers who ran away. I thought that was too much work. I thought that would never be me. I thought I could just wait where I was and hold tight until one day things changed. But all that waiting was actually running. Run, run, all I did was run.

Maybe now, at last, I could just be here. This was where I was supposed to be. This was *who* I was supposed to be.

It was getting close to the time my parents would get back. I pictured them coming in and seeing me in the dress. I felt an early wave of what I knew would be their discomfort—the anxiety and fear in their eyes, their fretful questions and their worried reassurances. What did it mean, what did it mean, it didn't matter what it meant.

For now I just wanted to flop down on the couch and relax.

After all, this was home.

Appendix

THE HALL OF ANCESTORS, CONTINUED

Some other ancestors, also hanging in the hall:

Flawless Sabrina. Alice Dunbar Nelson. Terry J. Long. Lorena Borjas. Chris Karabats. Cookie Mueller. Rebecca Rice. Lou Sullivan. James Dean. Crazy Owl. Montgomery Clift. Mark Morrisroe. Gloria Anzaldúa. Klaus Nomi. John Bernd. Maria Irene Fornes. Robert Duncan. John Cage and Merce Cunningham. Sappho. Tseng Kwong Chi. Barbara Gittings. Barbara Jordan. Socrates. Aimee Stephens. Alan Turing. Richard Bruce Nugent. Del Martin and Phyllis Lyon.

Hafiz. Ethyl Eichelberger. Michel Foucault. Deborah Sampson. Susan Sontag. Michael Dillon. Robert Vazquez-Pacheco. Rabbi Yochanan and Reish Lakish. Fae Richards, who stands for many, though she's a fiction. Jeff Weiss and Richard C. Martinez. Lou Reed. Dr. Julia Yasuda. Pete Burns. Greer Lankton. Wilmer "Little Ax" Broadnax. Kevin Killian. Reed Erickson. Michael Callen. Philip Johnson. Nelson Sullivan. Allen Ginsberg. Nero (oof). Hilma af Klint. Ms. Colombia. Roland Barthes. Layleen Xtravaganza Cubilette-Polanco. Lord Byron. Vito Russo. Arthur Russell. Fran Lebowitz. Peter Hujar. Tom and Alan, who lived across the street when Green was growing up, and who everyone called "roommates." Hylan. Mr. Irwin. Some of these people aren't dead yet, they held out hands and marked a way; friends asked Coco and Green to put them up. Don Yorty. Nicky Paraiso. The poet Tom Savage. Carmelita Estrellita. Katherine Meints, a math teacher. Mark Vannote, who buried many friends. Patrick Haggerty, who makes music. Kaki Dimock. Ranger Keith. Molly Malone Cook. Mary Oliver. Oh, and also Martin Wong. Melvin Dixon. David Bowie. Justin Chin. James Schuyler. José Esteban Muñoz. Jim Brodey. Cher.

Each time I visit Coco and Green, I catch a few more names.

Acknowledgments

This is a story about how we can't become ourselves living inside our own heads. We need other people who are willing to share their light with us and who are open to seeing ours, as we learn to find voice and expression for it.

What I'm trying to say is that some of these thank-yous are bigger than I have words for.

Thank you to my ancestors and my elders. And to my queer siblings.

Thank you, RJ Tolan, Joy Peskin, Elizabeth Lee, and Ross Harris.

Thank you, Clare Barron, Jordan Baum, Jeremy Bloom, Jonathan Chacón, Joshua Conkel, Patrick Costello, Kyle Dacuyan, Susan Dobinick, Jacob Eigen, Charles Ellenbogen, Ezra Furman, Charles Gariepy, Alice Gorelick, Paul Cameron Hardy, Nicholas Henderson, Eyad Houssami, Ricky Kelley, Binya Kóatz, Emma Lunbeck, Rae Mariah MacCarthy, Theo Motzenbacker, Eamon Murphy, Rachel Kauder Nalebuff, Chana Porter, Sakiko Sugawa, Ryan Szelong, and Korde Tuttle.

Among these are readers who responded to early drafts of the book, and friends who contributed personal ancestors to Coco and Green's hall.

Thank you, Chris. Thank you, Laura, Dad, and Mom.